I0725946

# The Cat's Paw

Kieran McNamara

This is a work of fiction. All of the characters, organizations, and events portrayed in this novel are either products of the author's imagination or are used fictitiously.

THE CAT'S PAW

Copyright © 2025 by Kieran McNamara
All rights reserved.
Images by Freepik
Fonts from Adobe

For more information, write
kieranmcnamaraauthor@yahoo.com

The moral right of the author has been asserted.
All rights reserved. No part of this book may be reproduced or transmitted by any person or entity, including internet search engines or retailers, in any form by any means, electronic or mechanical, including photocopying (except under the statutory exceptions provisions of the Australian Copyright Act 1968), recording, scanning, or by any information storage and retrieval system without the written permission of the author.

ISBN: 978-1-7641214-0-8 (trade paperback)

First edition: August 2025

A catalogue record for this book is available from the National Library of Australia

To my loving family: for your support and enthusiasm, I will always be grateful.

# Chapter 1



Harry turned to the sound of the voice, just as the ball struck him on the side of his face with a loud *WHACK* that knocked him to the ground. Bright lights flashed as his head kept spinning, and stars exploded like a fireworks celebration on the banks of the Potomac River on the 4th of July.

"Harry, are you okay?" A girl's voice came to him, her face wavering in and out until Stacey Edwards appeared. As his watery eyes cleared, her face seemed angelic, surrounded by the corona of the sun behind.

"Jeez, Potter, you're such a loser!"

Harry didn't need to see this face to know it was Brad Ogilvie, captain of the football team and self-confessed school bully, speaking to him as he bent down and picked up the offending ball.

"You should've caught it, ya loser," Brad sneered.

"Leave him alone, Brad," Stacey said, sounding like she meant business. "And his name is Porter for the thousandth time!"

Harry's dark hair and blue luminous eyes, rounded face with matching glasses, and light complexion all gave a likeness to the character who played the teenage wizard, although Daniel Radcliffe's eyes were supposed to be green, like in the books. Throughout the school years, his appearance had offered plenty of ammunition for never-ending taunting.

But Harry was 17 now; he was losing his boyish face and becoming a man—man enough to stand up to bullies.

"Hey, Stacey, whatcha doing with a loser like this?" Brad asked, scoffing.

Brad hadn't let go of a crush on Stacey since the start of grade one, and everyone at Rosedale High knew it. She had the deepest brown eyes to complement her long hair that curled in various shades of auburn. Though pretty enough to be part of the "in crowd," she didn't want to be a jock's girl, and certainly not Brad's.

"I'm fine, Stace, but thanks," Harry replied, his eyes clearing, but his husky voice had nothing to do with the ball hitting him. He and Stacey shared a bond so powerful you could almost touch it, despite them ever having mentioned it. Her look of relief and beautiful smile left him gasping for air, again not from the fall.

"Yo, Stacey, wanna come to the movies on Friday night?" Brad's words, on the other hand, were simply just less.

"Actually, I'm washing my hair." Stacey's look and tone clearly stated Brad's feelings weren't mutual.

The football star glowered down at Harry, and then walked off with a loud "Hurumph."

"He did that on purpose, you know," Stacey said, lightly squeezing Harry's arm with a slight break in her voice. They had known each other for ten years, and her concerned gaze suggested that they were now more than just study partners…

"I know, but it could as easily be seen as an accident if I retaliated," Harry said, trying to not read too much into her words and concern. Still…

Top scores in school suggested Harry was a bookworm, but these last few years had seen him grow physically and emotionally. The sudden loss of his father at an early age dictated his role as the substitute head of his family, forcing an early emotional development that made him seem older than his years.

They grabbed their bikes and headed for home, walking towards the north side of town.

Down the road a little, Harry asked, "What *are* you doing on Friday night, Stace?"

Stacey looked into his deep blue eyes. He was the sort of guy she would wait for forever, but she hoped he would return her affection sooner than that.

"Well, nothing really," she stammered.

"Want to come over to my place?" Harry's tone grew with confidence. They had hung out many times, often at the library or the diner, but it was always about schoolwork, never anything more.

"We could play some games, watch TV, or listen to music if you want to…?" Harry saw a light shining in Stacey's eyes and seemed to feel a response. "On Friday night," he finished with confidence.

"Like on a date?" was all Stacey could ask, her voice a mere whisper.

"Sure, a date." There it was: three words after more than ten years of a relationship that came close to something, but never actually delivered.

"We could order pizza, maybe cook or make something…" he swallowed hard and cleared his throat, now feeling edgy.

It felt like time had stopped, and every second was an eternity.

"I'd be thrilled." She put her hand in Harry's, and he felt the blood in his veins pump through every fiber of his body.

His racing heart hammered in his chest, and electricity poured through him.

They continued walking their bikes home, making small talk and planning to meet after school on Friday.

THREE DAYS!

That was what Stacey said to herself on her way home after parting ways on Tuesday afternoon. The sun was warm, the sky clear on a mid-summer afternoon, with birds chirping and kids playing in the street. It felt like a lifetime away!

She thought about what to wear, what to take, how to work it around her parents while hiding her growing excitement.

But on Friday at school, Harry gave her bad news. "My Mom is having a wicked bout of her arthritis. I need to be with her. I'm so sorry. Can I grab a rain check?"

Stacey's disappointment was harder to hide than she would've thought, but his reason was understandable.

"No problem," she replied. "Do you want to catch the movie matinee tomorrow? It's *Hansel and Gretel*."

"I have to clean out the backroom in the garage," Harry said. "I've been planning it for ages with Sam. Maybe we could get together Sunday?"

"Or I could help you in the garage?" Stacey offered. "I can get dropped off—say seven o'clock?"

"You're the best, Stace," Harry managed, trying to keep his voice steady, all the while choking on the inside.

# Chapter 2

Mike Porter had been a good man that worked hard and provided for his family whilst loving his car, a 1968 Ford Mustang Fastback he had restored and kept in the garage—his pride and joy. It was a classic ride and something that Harry kept close in his memory, since his father had died when he was only seven. He only had limited memories of his dad, but he thought about them regularly. And as for the car, that was a tradition he wanted to continue with a family of his own.

Though spared the cost of initially purchasing a car, Harry paid for gas, insurance, maintenance, and repairs. He was able to drive to work, tutor, and take Stacey home from late nights at the library study groups. He could also take his younger brother Sam to school and his mother to the doctor, shops, hairdresser, and the like.

Sam was almost the exact opposite of Harry, except for their matching bright blue eyes. He was fifteen, with shaggy blonde hair, rugged good looks, a muscular physique and outgoing boyish charm. Sam looked up to Harry more than just as a big brother—he idolized him without trying to let on about it.

Saturday morning had Harry up at first light, eager to get the job done, so maybe he and Stacey could go bike riding, picnicking, or bowling—actually anything except cleaning out their garage. He ate his breakfast and was finishing the washing up when Sam sauntered in, yawning over-exaggeratedly.

"Bro, do you always have to start your projects so early? It's like almost the middle of the night!" Sam's mouth gaped open again in a half real, yet half faked yawn, but he broke into a laugh when he saw Harry's eyes widen and him shake his head in disbelief.

"Oh, Sam," was all Harry could muster before he joined him, bursting out laughing.

Sam wolfed down his breakfast, and they made their way into the detached garage past the Mustang and into the dingy back room with a brick veneer and benches stacked with boxes of tools, newspapers, and jars filled with nuts, bolts, nails, screws, and pretty much anything and everything else.

"Right, so I've got some new packing boxes down here with electric lights. I reckon we make two piles—one of what we keep. The rest is rubbish to dump," Harry dictated.

They got the lights going and started making their way

through years of accumulation, gradually clearing benches and foot room. At exactly seven o'clock, Stacey arrived, dressed in old denim jeans and a dark green sweater, her hair in a ponytail and looking more gorgeous than ever but ready to get down to business and get her hands dirty. With the process of work explained, including Harry's rubbish protocol, the three of them set to work.

Several hours later, they stopped for a drink and a chocolate chip cookie, courtesy of Stacey's mum, Jody.

Sitting talking idly, Harry suddenly stood up, walked to the rear wall, and said, "Something isn't right here."

"You got that right, bro. It's a beautiful Saturday morning, and we're working for nuts. Well, nuts and bolts!" Sam laughed.

Stacey giggled at his pun.

"No, I mean, this wall looks different, and if I was outside, I'd say we weren't at the back of the shed yet." Harry was nothing, if not particular, but this was not a room either he or Sam frequented often. This was his dad's space that had become neglected, dusty, and home to more spiders and their webs than a deserted warehouse on the East end.

Stacey walked closer to investigate. "You know, the grout does look different for sure. Can we get more light and move this bench out from in front?"

Harry was on it, closely looking at the wall and then seeing a loose brick in the bottom corner. He grabbed a small pry bar and started levering it until it popped out. Sliding down until his face was on the floor, he grabbed the light and shone it into the hole.

"There's another wall, but further back!" he shouted.

"A secret room?" Sam asked. "What, like a crypt?" He laughed, but there was a nervous tinge to his voice.

"Maybe," Harry whispered. He looked at Sam and the two of them burst out laughing.

"You two!" Stacey said, exasperated.

The boys grabbed a hammer and chisel and set to work trying to lever out another brick, and then another, but the work was slow going.

"Wait up," Harry said. "If we keep going from the ground up, it's all going to end up collapsing. The problem is the higher we go, the harder the mortar. There must've been water on the floor at some point to loosen that bottom one."

"Good work, Sherlock, but what are we going to do now?" Sam asked.

"Maybe we need better tools, like you know, bigger hammers?" Stacey suggested, now more than a little intrigued.

"Yep, and you know what they say," Harry quipped as he crossed to a workbench filled with power tools and pulled out a Kanga hammer drill. "When the going gets tough…"

"The tough get earplugs," Sam finished with a laugh, and he went looking for them. Shortly after, with a power lead, safety switch, dust masks, and earplugs, they were in business.

It was a noisy, dusty, and dirty job, but the bricks began to fall.

Forty-five minutes later, Harry called a break so they could ascertain the situation. Almost a third of the wall was down. The room looked like a demolition site coal mine had exploded, and there was quite a pile of bricks. Sam and Harry had taken turns on the Kanga while Stacey had brought drinks and searched for things to help. She'd found a couple of large buckets to carry the bricks out, goggles, rags to wrap their hair and anything that could be considered a light—lanterns, torches, and another electric lamp. It was becoming quite the project, and the three of them rotated using the drill, picking up bricks, and sweeping up the mess.

That all stopped when a voice from the distance sung out. "Helllloooo. Can I come in?" a female called from the front of the garage next door.

*The garage—uh-oh! The Mustang!* Harry thought. *It better not be covered with dust...*

He yanked the door open and passed the Ford to the main roller door where their fifteen-year-old neighbor Bethany Carlson was happily inviting herself in.

"Hello, Harry," she said, greeting him casually. "That's quite some work you've got going on by the sound of it. Are you building a new shed or just tearing this one down?"

Her question was polite enough—searching, wondering, but not mocking.

"Gidday, Beth," Harry replied. "No, just making a little change in the back there. I'm going to move Dad's—I mean my

Mustang out for now. Sam's in the room out back if you want to go for a look, but it's a bit dusty." He wasn't sure if asking her to join them was the right move, but he wasn't sure he could stop her, either.

"Oh, that's alright, I'm not scared of a little dust," she said, as she sidled her way past the Fastback, intrigued by the growing noise of *hhhhhrrrrrhhh, hhhhhrrrrrhhh, hhhhhrrrrrhhh* blaring louder as she neared the door between the garage and the storeroom.

Stepping through, she saw Stacey and Sam busy at work demolishing a brick wall.

"Oh hey, Stacey, how's it going?" she yelled over the noise of the Kanga. Bethany knew Stacey enough to say hello, but not much more, with almost two years between them.

"Uh, hi, Beth, what's going on?" Sam jumped in, stopped drilling, and wiped the sweat from his brow with a rag.

"Hello, Sam." Beth was Sam's age and shared classes with him, so they knew each other. She was neither overly tall nor short for her age, had shoulder length black hair with the slightest curl, and a fair complexion with the deepest green eyes that glistened like emeralds shining in the sun.

Sam and Stacey filled Beth in on what had been happening and how, with the dust clearing and additional light, they could now see what looked like an old well in the cavity behind the wall.

After pulling the car out and covering it, Harry returned to see Sam stuttering and a bit off his normal game. Beth had always been civil and yet stand-offish to Sam, who had tried to woo her years ago. But that was not going to deter him now. The teenage Casanova Samuel Porter was quickly regaining his composure.

"You see, Beth, there has to be a reason this wall was put up. And we can work out when that was, roughly, if we just think about it. And we can put up a temporary wall if it's a safety issue—you know, with scaffolds and stuff like plastic wall. I've seen it before. You can help, but if you don't want to go getting all dirty, we men can handle this…"

Harry smiled inwardly, then looked up and caught the same look from Stacey, and the two of them burst into laughter.

"What's so funny?" Sam blushed, knowing he was trying too hard. The problem was, he actually really liked Beth. Her eyes hypnotized him, no less than a snake handler entranced by a rattlesnake in a bazaar in Cairo.

"Nothing. Let's see what's going on back here, shall we?" Harry grinned as he led the way forward through the broken-down wall with a battery-powered lantern, the others close behind.

The air was damp and cool, the dust had barely settled, and there was a heavy atmosphere in the newly dubbed "Well Room."

Harry's muscles tightened, and the tendons pulsated in his neck as he unfastened the second top button of his shirt. He felt a trickle of sweat down his spine despite noticing a drop in temperature from the storeroom. Of course, none of them would admit anything was too unnerving, especially the boys.

The walls in the well-room were brick veneer again, but the brick of the well did not seem to match the rest of the walls at all. Beth felt cold and clammy, shivering noticeably.

"It's like the bricks are hundreds of years older," Stacey whispered with a tremor. She felt somewhat shaky and noticed Sam's forehead was beading with sweaty chills.

"Why are you whispering?" Sam whispered back. They looked at each other and burst out laughing, alleviating their apprehension.

But they all secretly wondered why the well would have been bricked in. To hide it?

Two timbers rose as uprights out of the circular brick wall, made of rudimentary hardwood with a crossbeam to match and old plate tiles. There was a rusty iron turnstile with a wooden handle, and the crossbeam had an old rope that disappeared into the dark abyss of the well.

"Forget hundreds. It's like a thousand years old," Beth said.

There was little else in the room. An old bench backed onto what must've been the real back wall of the garage. The floor was dirt, not concrete, and the ceiling exposed beams to the center apex. Stacey had the feeling of the bench resembling an aging pew, and the hardwood beams of an old church came to mind.

"So, are we going to wind the bucket up?" Sam asked what they were all thinking. He inched forward towards the well and heard a metallic click as he stood on something.

"It's a keychain," he said, picking it up. "It's a Ford."

"Jeepers, that's Dad's!" Harry gasped as he examined it. It was just a cheap trinket, an old Ford Mustang tag that must've cost three bucks. "We gave it to him for his thirtieth birthday. I remember Mom helping me buy it." He took a moment before finishing. "I was five." He stuttered out the last words, saddened by his memory, but acutely aware that this meant his father had been on the inside of the wall at some point. He had to have known about the well!

Stacey stood directly behind him and grabbed his left hand, clasping it firmly.

Harry gently squeezed her arm in appreciation, her smile enough for him as Stacey tightened her grip.

"Okay, so Dad was here." Sam tried taking the initiative, although he was just five when his father died and wouldn't have remembered the gift of the keychain occurring two years earlier than that. "He probably saw it as a danger and sealed it off."

"Yeah, you know, to stop nosy boys falling in," Beth chipped in, trying to lighten the mood.

"Exactly—it could mean anything." Stacey clasped her arms around herself now. It was like the air had grown frosty, in spite of an early summer's day outside.

"So, we have a consensus to wind the winch?" Harry wanted to be sure they all agreed, but either way, he'd go ahead alone, even if the others didn't agree.

"Yes, absolutely." Sam bounced up and down on his toes, speaking louder than he needed and leaning forward to peer inside the well.

"Sure," Beth agreed, nodding.

"No question." Stacey was becoming more assertive, convinced that this was the right move, but she couldn't explain the unnatural coldness that seemed to wrap its icy fingers over her shoulders.

HARRY STARTED WINDING THE WINCH. IT WAS EASY AT FIRST, but got harder as it climbed. It creaked with rusty grinding, the rope wrenching on itself with every turn, gradually pulling up whatever cargo it might contain from the depths below. He continued to put more effort in, but it had the opposite effect, slowing the ascent. Next up, Sam took a turn but eventually passed the crank handle to Beth.

Beth was well-built, muscular, and a gym-junkie. She loved working out, and it showed, but before long she had to pass the handle to Stacey, who then, in turn, had to hand it back over to Harry. It seemed to take forever—winding gears grinding and rope creaking until at last a wooden pail with metal bands emerged from the darkness of the shaft.

"There's something in it!" Sam shouted, peering in from the edge.

"Maybe a Hobbit?" Beth quipped, catching Sam's eye with a

broad smile.

"Bring it up!" Sam laughed, enjoying her humor and the look.

"Easy, we don't want to tip it over," Stacey said from beside him, straining forward.

With one last crank of the handle, Harry heaved it up and over the top of the well. They all gasped at what they saw. Inside was a simple oil lamp.

"What the…?" Sam was incredulous; all that effort but with so little result.

"It's so pretty!" Stacey exclaimed.

Harry was panting and sweating from the exertion, but more mystified than disappointed with the contents. *How could it have taken so much, and gotten so heavy, with so little weight? It's like it didn't want to come up!* he thought, more than a little confused.

"Is that real gold?" Beth asked, peering closely.

"I was at least hoping for a bucket of gold doubloons, cast ingots, or 100 carat diamonds," Sam muttered, but the others were clearly enthralled with their prize.

The lamp was about eight and a half inches in length, gold in color, with small, embedded jewels: embellishments and ornate engravings that reminded Stacey of ancient writing and hieroglyphics. It had a handle, a lid, and a spout, and a small hole in front of the handle.

*OMG I'm in Arabian Nights!* Harry thought ridiculously.

"It's really old," Stacey said.

"It's really cool," Beth chipped in.

"I think the hole is for a key." Harry now had a closer inspection of the lamp.

"Well, I think we should give it a jolly good rub and see what sort of genie pops out, old boy!" Sam gave it his best Cockney accent with a wide grin. The tension broke, and they all burst out laughing.

"You know that hole is a funny shape—not hexagonal exactly, but convex hexagonal maybe." Harry was thinking out loud.

It wasn't lost on Sam. "Are you a walking encyclopedia?" He laughed. "I've never even heard of a convex hexagonal."

"Yeah, it's a little unusual because the sides aren't all exactly even, but a hexagon all the same." The joke was lost on Harry as he mulled over the earlier clean-up. "I saw some key-type tools in a drawer earlier."

"So, we're not going to give it a rub?" Sam quipped. He gave Beth a wide smile and a wink.

"Samuel Porter, that sort of talk will get you nowhere!" Beth said, but turned her head to avoid sharing her smile. He was just so exasperatingly Sam!

They went back through the broken wall into the room off the garage, all noting the mess that still remained to be cleaned up. Or the brick wall to be rebuilt. Harry wondered if he was going to have to turn his hand to masonry.

Going to a bench with drawers on the side wall, he opened the second drawer down and grabbed two handfuls of small tools, mostly Hex keys but with an assortment of others. They looked like they were a mixture of different sets, old but not ancient.

"There's more in there," he said as Sam jumped in, emptying the drawer.

"Let's have a look." Sam gave him a gentle shove.

They lay the tools on top of the bench with Sam humming until Harry gave a good-natured nudge back. But after a few minutes, they realized there was nothing to match the convex hexagonal of the lamp.

"Maybe it's not a keyhole?" Beth surmised.

"Or it's in another drawer?" Sam started opening and shutting the drawers again.

"Or at the bottom of the well?" Stacey voiced what they had all thought but didn't want to consider.

"What am I missing?" Harry said.

"Maybe you need time to think about that," Stacey said.

"Yeah, like with pizza." Sam was always happy to be thinking about food.

"Or Chinese," Harry countered, knowing it was Stacey's favorite. "How about that rain check?"

"What, now?" Stacey asked, looking down at her dusty clothes and imagining what her hair and face looked like…

"No, I'll run you home, then pick you up at 5.00 o'clock?" Harry checked his watch.

"Sounds amazing." Stacey grinned.

As they headed out, Stacey asked Beth if she was coming

back in the morning.

"Absolutely," she said, with her eyes gleaming. "I wouldn't miss this for the world."

"So same bat time?" Sam's eye twinkled.

"Same bat channel!" Beth replied with a giggle.

*OMG,* Sam thought. *This girl is full of surprises!* His eyes brightened, and he laughed.

# Chapter 3

Jonathon Edwards was a Real Estate Mogul and at six foot five inches, was more than a little intimidating. Harry had met him on several occasions, and things were formally cordial, but he let out a sigh of relief as his tension released, glad it was Jody Edwards who opened the door when he went to collect Stacey a couple of hours later.

"Well, hello, Harry, come right on in," she greeted him. "Stacey is just freshening up and won't be but a minute. Can I get you a soda, or maybe a hot chocolate chip cookie? I've just taken them out of the oven…"

"One of your home chocolate chip cookies would be outstanding. Thanks, Mrs. E." Harry enjoyed the simplicity of life that was Mrs. Edwards, in spite of their obvious wealth.

As she got him a cookie, they small-talked about the weather and school, nothing special.

"These are absolutely awesome as ever, Mrs. E." Harry's praise was no lie.

"Well, they should be dear. You've helped me refine the recipe," Jody replied. "So, what are your plans tonight?"

"Oh, you know, nothing dramatic; play some music, talk shop, grab some takeout, bring her home by ten thirty if that's okay?"

"Well, I'm no pumpkin, babe." A voice reached out to him.

Harry turned to see Stacey had come down the stairs behind them, wearing a red dress with spaghetti straps and blue denim jacket with matching jewel studded cowboy boots to the knees. Her hair was long and wavy, and she only wore minimal make-up to accentuate her features. She was stunning, and Harry felt under-dressed in blue jeans, white graphic tee, and Panda Air Jordans.

"Wow," he gasped, followed by a "wow, indeed" from Jody.

"So, let's get moving, shall we?" Stacey said.

"Sure. You look absolutely gorgeous," he managed to stammer out, feeling rattled to his bones.

"Not so bad yourself. Let's go."

Stacey gave her mum a kiss on the cheek, held her arm out for Harry to take, and left no less formally than if for the Prom.

They picked up takeout, and the drive back to the Porter's place on Old Mill Road was filled with jovial banter along with the aromas of Chinese from Ken's Wok. Passing out orders to

Sam and their mom, Regina, they spent the next couple of hours playing music and talking light-heartedly while eating. At the bottom of the bag were two fortune cookies, and Harry handed one to Stacey, smiling. She opened it and laughed, quoting, "To know the road ahead, ask those coming back."

Harry opened his and read, "The key to the future lies in the past." He looked up at Stacey, cogs turning and gears whirring as he thought about what he was sure was a key belonging to the newly acquired lamp.

Then his face brightened as the penny dropped and he half-shouted, "Be right back!" dashing from the room.

Two minutes later, while Stacey was wondering just how long he was going to be, Harry burst back in.

"I've got it! It was on the keychain in the Mustang—the one with the keys, not the one with the medallion that Sam found. It's been here all this time, just hanging with the keys—a small tool I've seen a thousand times and never wondered about!"

Harry held his hand out. On the keychain was a small tool held by a hole in the top, barely an inch and a quarter long, with a convex hexagonal end on it. It was metal, but old like iron. They marveled at the find, but before they knew it, Harry's watch beeped and he jumped up in surprise.

"Tempus Fugit," he said. "We'd better start making a move, or you'll be late, and your dad will make pumpkin pie out of me!"

"Temp what?" Stacey was lost.

"Time flies," he said, quoting a Latin proverb with his

boyish grin.

Soon after, as they were heading back to Stacey's place, he put his hand over hers, saying, "I'm glad you're my girl, Stace."

She smiled back, turning to face him and squeezed his hand in response. "I'm glad too, Harry."

Standing on the porch shortly afterwards, Harry said, "I had a really great time."

"Me too," she replied with her million-dollar smile. "Seven o'clock again?"

"You really are the bestest, Stace." Harry was a good four inches taller than her. He bent forward and kissed her gently but firmly on the lips.

Stacey gasped inwardly, tipping her head back and closing her eyes while she held his kiss. Her arms circled him, and her hands held the small of his back as the world started to spin.

Breaking apart at last, she gasped, laughing euphorically.

"See you at seven!" Harry called out, leaping off the porch like Spiderman but without the web and suit, waiting only to make sure she went inside safely before jumping into the Mustang and heading for home.

EARLY SUNDAY MORNING, HARRY WAS FINISHING BREAKFAST when Sam joined him. "So, how did it go, Romeo?"

Putting aside his experience during the night, Harry was jubilant in his reply. "It was awesome! Better than that. It was phenomenal! She's so great!"

"Bro, I meant the Chinese food!" Sam laughed.

Harry smiled and then laughed in spite of himself.

Sam was the ultimate likable beach surfer—except he didn't surf! Laid-back and easy going, he was smart in spite of the persona he presented. Extremely good looking, he could date almost any girl and could make class president without even running. But Sam's revere of his older brother was definitely reciprocal. They shared an incredibly strong emotional bond.

Bouncing off the walls with how the date had gone, Harry moved on to the chore at hand.

"Let's do this!" Harry half yelled, clearly pumped.

After Stacey arrived, she and Harry showed the newly found key to Sam and Beth.

"No way!" Sam shouted. "It was there all the time."

Harry asked again for a second consensus. "Okay, so we have to agree on this," he started.

Sam interrupted. "We are definitely doing this! Right, dudes?"

Stacey looked at Sam directly, held his stare, then turned to Harry. "We are absolutely doing this."

Beth looked at Sam, replying, "Yes, Kemosabe," quoting the Lone Ranger, smirking.

Harry grinned in reply.

"Casting vote again, bro." Sam looked at Harry for confirmation.

"Yeah, no pressure." Harry felt somewhat pressured, nonetheless. He now knew that his father had known about the well, and that he might've known about the wall, if not having built it. He definitely knew about the key and consequently had to have known about the lamp.

But if he knew about the lamp, why was it at the bottom of an old well?

"Okay, let's do this." Harry inserted it into the lamp and turned it clockwise.

There was a slight clunk, like gears moving, and they all held their breath.

The air thickened, and time seemed to slow. Sam looked at Harry, who looked at Stacey. She, in turn, looked at Beth. The day had become surreal—a mixture of reality and fantasy. The room shimmered like the mirage in a boiling hot desert, then a misty fog appeared.

GRADUALLY THE AIR CLEARED, AND ON A STOOL IN THE CORNER sat a man, bare chested with bright green three-quarter pants, his dark skin displaying an array of even darker tattoos over his body. He had a clean-shaven head and face with a chiseled look and darkly sunken eyes of jet-black coal. On his arms, he sported large golden arm bracelets like the kind Roman Centurions wore in the Colosseum, which were matched with a large golden necklace.

The words of an old song Harry's mom used to listen to res-onated; something about darkness being an old friend.

The stranger had an ominous look, foreboding and full of darkness. Whoever this guy was, he was not of this world.

# Chapter 4

"Oh-hum, so hi there," Sam greeted him, trying to hold fast to being the entertainer, the class clown.

The girls stood back, but Harry—this new self-assured and full of confidence Harry—fronted up to the stranger, ignoring warning looks from Stacey.

"Humans." The stranger lowered his head in an opposing gaze, his voice guttural, dispassionate, and unforgiving.

"Maybe, but I'm pretty sure we just freed you from that lamp." Harry's words resonated a conviction none of the others were familiar with.

"Freedom, yes, that gives you three opportunities, Master." The stranger's voice was as cold as ice.

Harry gave it some thought. Ideas came and went, but he immediately dismissed them as mere childhood dreams. Then he wondered about the history of the stranger. A past that could direct the future, maybe…

"You allude to the promise of opportunity." Harry's voice was deep and controlled. "We want to know your name and why the bucket becomes heavier the higher we raise it; can we lift anything from below and return it from up here as easily?"

The questions bewildered the other teens, but Harry was determined. The heaviness of the bucket as it neared the top mystified him, and he didn't know if it related to the lamp, the stranger, or maybe even a doorway that could send objects, or even people from here to there—wherever there was—and back.

"It's nothing too hard—no gold or jewels required to magically appear—just a simple question, nothing too onerous," he finished.

"Your wish is my command." The stranger rose, looked straight down a good seven inches at Harry, staring him directly in the eyes. "My name is Jinni, Master Harry," he said contemptuously.

Harry was both surprised and disappointed by his answer, but Stacey knew that his question had been answered—but just the first and easiest part. The stranger had given his name, after all, as asked.

She jumped in, realizing Harry was testing this "Genie" to see if he was for real. "It's okay, Jinni. We are simply seeking answers as to how you have come to join us. And our questions mean no disrespect."

"Yes, Jinni; isn't that the Arabic name for Genie?" Harry asked. "Persian?"

"Yes, Master Harry. You are aware," the stranger replied.

"Maybe," Harry admitted. He realized they could end up with no answers to this. Even if there were truly three fairytale wishes to be granted, they could be deceived into receiving nothing at all. He had the hardest decision of his life ahead of him.

But then Stacey jumped in again, surprising them all. "So, do we need to say we wish for a wish to be granted, or does just saying we want to, like, know your name, count as a wish?"

The stranger looked at her intently. Harry was impressed, and Sam stared wide-eyed, even more in awe.

"Would you like proof of my wishes?" he asked. "What if I was to show you the bottom of the well, or even the portal as Master Harry suspects?"

This one made them look at each other in surprise, as Harry hadn't mentioned any portal. *But I was thinking about a doorway,* Harry thought.

"Or would you all rather I grant a room of gold bullion, doubloons and jewels: treasures unsurpassed that would have you rich beyond your wildest dreams, as Master Sam desires?" Jinni's eyes glowed like molten gold, his voice elevated, and he rose up, seeming to grow two, three, four feet above them, swirling in fog.

"Or what if you were to show their father's death," Stacey simply said.

"It would be a show of faith?" Beth offered.

Their visitor didn't say a word, but the air filled with the heaviness of a dream, a mystic surreal that could be a virtual reality in a video game with a headset taking you out of the real world and into the impossible.

There was a man in a swirling aurora, a strong, assertive man with long, dark hair and a muscular physique dressed in overalls with no sleeves. They weren't looking at a screen, but almost looking down from above, like gods in an Olympian arena. The man went to work in a garage, under a car; perhaps changing a brake shoe or similar part inside the rear wheel lying on a flat trolley. The swirling came and went, and then there was a new shape, something ominous.

It came from the darkness: first one, then another, and then a third. The new shapes became forms, some like human but not human, others like dogs, but not dogs: forms that materialized to dogs and then attacked the man under the car. They dragged him out from under the vehicle, taking turns attacking him over and over until their overwhelming power left him lying mauled and mutilated, succumbing to a horrible death.

Harry looked on as the swirling air subsided, as did any evidence of what had happened to his father and the "things" in the vision. The true fate of his father was no accident.

"Why?" was all he could say.

The Jinni replied to his question with a fair gaze. "There are creatures that will graze upon whatever prey they are set upon, Master."

"People," Harry said, choking.

"Yes, Master Harry, animals, people. Their flesh doesn't discriminate. The Grimole and their Borgil appear from the darkness, attack, and disappear again. They consider entire worlds theirs to pillage and plunder, and their appetite is insatiable."

"And this well is a gateway to those other worlds?" Harry asked.

"Other worlds and other dimensions, yes, Master Harry," he replied.

"One my father discovered?"

"Yes, again, Master Harry."

Harry thought about that for a minute. "That's why my father was so intent on keeping it buried, along with the lamp." Harry thought of his father and how he was killed. He was desperate to know more, and yet knowing scared him. And it was only starting to make sense. Terrifying sense.

"Yes, such a noble deed. He wanted to keep his world safe." Now there was a note of respect to his voice.

"Show us more, Jinni." Stacey wanted actual proof as much as the others. "My wish is that Harry and Sam's mother, Regina, is cured of her arthritis."

"Your wish is my command, Mistress Stacey," the stranger confirmed.

The four teens looked at each other, knowing they were going to have to prove if the Jinni's abilities were real, or not. And if these abilities were real, this used up another wish, their second.

With that, Harry led them into the house to check on his mother, who greeted them with the smell of home-made pizza. Lunchtime was due, and it seemed like a lifetime since breakfast, so they made short work of Regina's cooking.

Regina was upbeat, bustling around the kitchen, asking about this and that, taking plates and serving her guests.

"She's having a great day," Stacey commented when she was out of earshot.

"Like cured, and the wish is granted?" Harry said.

It was exactly like that.

THE STRANGER REMAINED IN THE ROOM OFF THE GARAGE, SIT-ting on the stool in a dark corner waiting patiently for their return.

"Now you believe?" he asked, still somewhat scornfully.

"Maybe. Will you share your story with us?" Harry requested, feeling uncertain he might be pushing the boundaries. "Enlighten us of the worlds beyond Earth?"

The Jinni stared into Harry's eyes and replied thoughtfully.

"I am from an age of a millennium long past," he started. "I am of the Arhmeic, the mystic, born to show and for others to follow. Jinni is not my birth name, but the name given to my kind. My true name is Wazeem. I am now the last of my people."

Harry paused and then drove the nail home they all wanted to know. "How did you become imprisoned in the lamp?"

Harry was starting to bond with the stranger, and the others waited patiently, listening without interruption.

"It was treachery, Master Harry. Nothing I shouldn't have seen coming, but treachery all the same." Wazeem's gaze wandered for the first time distantly, recalling events of many lifetimes ago.

Again, the air filled with the mystic eeriness, the swirling clouds of past events and then a man appeared, not dissimilar to the tattooed giant before them, but shorter and rounder, older and dressed in bright yellow bloomers, a white linen shirt, and purple vest with a long scimitar at his hip. His bright blue satin sash on his waist matched the turban with the purple of the vest intertwined. The man held the lamp up and stood in gold and gems knee-deep, laughing gleefully with a very unnaturally psychotic look—laughing, laughing, laughing…

"My brother, Helsar," the Jinni said, "found the lamp and worked out that it needed a prisoner to empower the holder." He paused and then finished quietly, "I was that prisoner."

The room stayed silent as they tried to comprehend what Wazeem was saying. His own brother had imprisoned him.

WITH TIME GETTING LATE, BETH SAID GOODBYE AS HARRY AND Sam dropped Stacey home.

It was well after six o'clock and getting dark. Harry walked Stacey up the path to the front door, continuing the discussion of the day's events on the car ride over, amongst Sam's light-hearted banter trying to keep spirits high.

"See you tomorrow," Stacey said without question.

Harry gave her a gentle kiss on the lips. "Pick you up at seven." He smiled, before leaving with Sam to return home.

They took Wazeem up the back stairs to Harry's room where he sat on an aging armchair by the window. The boys nibbled on some leftovers, but the Arhmeic did not want to eat or drink. In fact, he did not seem to sleep.

Just before the sun started to rise, Harry went downstairs where his mother was in the kitchen cooking eggs, toast, and pancakes for breakfast.

"What are you doing up?" He couldn't believe what she was doing. At 5.30am? And cooking breakfast? "You seem good?" Harry said, snagging a piece of French toast.

"Better than good, I feel like I haven't in many years," she replied with a wide smile.

Wazeem had done it. *He really had done it!*

Returning upstairs, Harry noticed Wazeem was not in the armchair, so he ventured outside to the detached garage. There was a freezing coldness that was not of the morning air, and the further he ventured, the icier it grew. Stepping through the broken wall, he found Wazeem next to the well.

"This is a very dangerous place, isn't it, Wazeem?" he asked.

"Yes, Master Harry. It could undo all of the goodness you have here," he replied.

They both knew he was alluding to the future of mankind.

Harry paused, and the silence was heavy. "I want to use my final opportunity, Wazeem." Harry's voice cracked a little. "My wish is that your freedom is granted, and you be exonerated forthwith."

Wazeem stared into Harry's eyes, gridlocked. "You would do that for me, Master?"

"Yes, Wazeem. You were incarcerated for the crime of being a good brother and nothing more. We can only help you find simple things in this world, but I hope you will find your own way here, or wherever you may venture. Knowing of my father's death and curing my mother's illness are worth a thousand times your release. Thank you for granting these opportunities."

Wazeem's look was a reflection of gratitude, and Harry sensed a difference as to how the Stranger had regarded him previously, maybe even showing some regret at trying to fool him with the earlier use of a supposed wish to just reveal his name.

*Are we even at two, or three wishes used?* Harry wondered, now unsure.

Morning saw them together again and discussing the events of the previous days, with Harry explaining what he had done with what he thought was their final wish.

"What do we do with the lamp?" Sam asked.

"Who bricked up the wall and why?" Stacey added. "And

what good is that now with the lamp here?"

"And what good does a brick wall do against 'out-worldly' creatures?" Beth countered.

"What are even 'out-worldly' creatures?" Stacey asked.

"Dad knew about the well and had a key to the lamp. How did this relate to him and his death?" Sam kept going, like a hound on the scent.

"Okay, this is getting way out of control. Let's do these one at a time," Harry said. "First, the lamp. We're going to keep it here until we figure out more about its relationship with Wazeem and Dad."

They all agreed on that one.

"Second, the wall. Wazeem?" Harry looked to the Genie.

"The wall protects the well but only physically," Wazeem replied. "It was rebuilt after your father died."

*There it is!* Harry thought.

"Okay, that takes care of the well itself but not of the 'out-world' it contains," he said, now thinking about his mother's knowledge of the well, his father's death, and her involvement with the wall to conceal the well.

"I had the power to hold them back as long as I was bound to the lamp," the Jinni replied.

"So, the wall and the well have no bearing on it?" Sam asked.

"Correct, Master Sam."

"Who is them?" Harry asked the Genie.

"We are different, but still of your kind," he explained. "We are joint to this universe, so consider us 'off-world.'"

"As opposed to…?" Stacey asked.

"These things that come to acquire your bodies are not of this world. They are of another dimension - not an off-world but an out-world," Wazeem stated.

"So, the wall really was put there for our protection? Okay, that doesn't make sense. How could a brick wall really keep us safe?" Sam asked.

"Because we were kids, and it stopped us accessing the well—and the lamp," Harry replied. He realized it was a physical barrier for when they were young, protecting them from not just falling into the well, but what access to it really meant.

Sam frowned deeply. "So now that we're no longer bound to it, a whole new universe of bad things can get in, right from our garage!" His voice grew weak as he realized that the wall was real, but insignificant to the doorway, or portal which really kept these worlds and "dimensions" apart.

"Uh-oh and double uh-oh," Beth added, also coming to grips with it.

"No matter." Wazeem's voice deepened as he rose off the stool, standing a full six foot eleven inches. "Humans have given me something I've not known in eons: trust, freedom, and cama-raderie. I have no brothers to embrace now, no women to bear young, nowhere to go with this liberation after half an eternity of imprisonment. I shall stay with you and help fight off these creatures of the darkness using the tools of the esoteric sorcery from my forefathers and the remaining Guardians!" Wazeem thundered out the last words with force that shook the room.

*He's like Gandalf!* Harry thought of the white wizard in awe. But words were only words. What tools was he referring to?

"We are grateful for your…" Harry started to say when there was a screeching howl from the room containing the well. The howling was joined by a second, and then a third. There was an air of excitement to them, like hyenas bringing down their prey.

The teens all looked at each other and then at Wazeem, wide-eyed as the iciness crawled across their skin like tentacles stretching out from the depths of the well below.

"Borgil!" Wazeem shouted. "The vampire hounds of the Grimorium!"

Sam thought that his bladder might let go.

# Chapter 5

Now free, Wazeem started citing ritual in an ancient tongue. It was a deeply voiced chant that sounded like an electric toothbrush rotating on the back teeth of his mouth, throaty but with a harmonious tone.

*"Awededoor-delaydah comeloo leymaydoo*
*Awesemayilsa Dehemarcemare"*

*(Definition):*
*"We the Su-dah are the Guardians of the universe,*
*Now call forth the Lygard to vanquish and disperse."*

Shapes swirled around them, circling the room, but it was impossible to define what they were. Then the shapes—three maybe—flew from the well room, and a low growling echoed from within the depths of the well. The screeching wail of the unseen beasts receded and then disappeared altogether.

Before the teens could relax, Wazeem said, "We have forced them back for now, but they will return."

"Well, that's just great," Beth said, staring at Sam.

"What are the Lygard?" Harry didn't miss a beat. Whatever they were, he was thankful they'd be showing up.

"They are the faithful servants of Sudin Duhlion," Wazeem said, somewhat emotionally. "They are the lions who fight and die for their Masters. The Lygard are true Su-dah!"

Grimole, Borgil, Lygard, Su-dah! All these new words intrigued him, and Harry wanted to know more. "And the Sudin Duhlion is your creed?"

Wazeem looked back with something like amazement. *How could this mortal be so aware of what things were, what are, and what could be? He is but a boy!*

"Yes, Master Harry," the off-worlder replied. "And I believe the human leaders are ready to learn the ways of old—ancient ways that have long been protected and will open your eyes."

Human leaders. They all picked up on that reference to their position despite their having no political status, let alone notability.

Wazeem took a step back, opened his arms, and raised his head. He started reciting that ancient tongue, creating a small whirlwind that turned and spun, but all the while obeying his control, remaining directly in front of him.

"Walk into the eddy, Master Harry," he commanded.

Harry stepped forward, exhilarated as he was carried upwards, lifted by forces of the unknown.

"Now accept your union with the elements—the gift of Fire and Water."

Harry was lowered to the ground when Wazeem again recited the ancient tongue, recreating the wind and saying, "Rise, Mistress Stacey."

She walked forward and was carried upward, as Wazeem's words resonated. "Your new bond is with the cosmos of life: Space and Healing."

Stacey glided to the ground, feeling slightly dizzy.

"Enter, Master Sam." Another vortex swirled, and Sam felt excitement at the change as Wazeem chanted, "You shall become one with the forces of the World, with the power of Speed and Strength."

Sam almost bounced off the ground in his effort to step into the vortex.

Lastly, Beth approached the swirling gust. As she eyed it with concern, Wazeem took her hand and led her forward until she was carried upward, with the Genie's words reverberating.

"Merge with Nature, young Mistress Beth, for Time and Form belong to you."

Beth levitated down, feeling very relieved.

Harry looked around at them, noticing changes immediately.

Stacey seemed older, wiser and more confident. Sam was bigger, bolder, and larger than life—more than usual, that was. Beth was buoyant, almost euphoric, on high-octane and exhilarated.

The wind fizzled out, and they continued to eye each other.

"Phew," Sam puffed out overly exaggerated. "Well, that was something different." He looked across at Beth and thought he saw a new look—was that admiration?

"Tell us more about where the Grimole come from, please?" Stacey asked Wazeem.

"The *where* they come from is very different to what you know, Mistress Stacey. In the devil's place there are different laws of physics to what you know, see, hear, feel, and touch. They are but shapes that do not have form. They can appear and disappear instantly, and they move at lightning speed because time and space are so different. It is an out-world to your world, another dimension."

"Out-world, but not off-world." Stacey got it. "Then how can they be killed?"

The question caught Harry off-guard, the hardness of her voice something new to him.

"When they come through the gate to other worlds, the rules of nature also change. When they arrive on Earth, they are much slower and solid because they assume real form. Solid bodies that die like anything else. It just takes time for the effects of Earth to slow them."

"*Killable,*" Stacey said coldly. This was definitely a new side to her.

"Okay, so time for lunch." Sam was always hungry, and today was no exception, out-worldly demons, off-worldly Genies, and the like, or not.

"Yes, and I think Wazeem should meet Mom now," Harry said, looking at him. "Do you think you can rustle up some 21st Century Earth clothes and join us?"

"Yes, Master Harry," he replied with what could've been mistaken for a half-smile.

"And maybe drop the Master in public?" Harry grinned.

Wazeem snapped his fingers, and his clothes changed. He fronted a U2 t-shirt, camel brown chinos, and black boots.

"Wow yeah, dude," Sam said.

They exited the garage and crossed the lawn to find Regina working in the garden.

"Oh, Mom." Sam could not believe it. She was in a floral dress, wearing a wide-brim hat with gardening gloves on a mat, and had pulled out a pile of weeds and flowers she had cut back. Her cheeks were rosy with color that hadn't been there in many years. Her frailness had disappeared, and with naturally blonde hair and deep blue eyes she looked positively stunning.

"Oh, good morning," she greeted them.

"Hey, Mom, this is Wazeem, a...friend of ours." Friend seemed easier to explain than what: Guardian? Samaritan? Salvation?

"Well, good morning, Wazeem," Regina greeted him politely.

"I was just going to wash up and organize some lunch, if you'd like to join us?" She didn't seem fazed by his looming size or presence.

He returned with the most courteous manners. "That would be most generous of you, Mistress Regina."

Regina blushed and mumbled that he didn't have to be so formal.

They went inside, and a half hour later were busy making and eating fresh ham and chicken rolls with salad and mayonnaise. The mood was light; Sam was jovial, Regina buoyant, and Wazeem was even able to smile. After the main, Regina brought out some apple pie she had made that morning, with whipped cream. The afternoon sun streamed into the kitchen as Harry sat beside Stacey, holding hands. They had all finished eating, except for Sam of course, who always wanted seconds. And thirds, or sometimes even fourths…

Harry quizzed his mother about the loss of his father many years ago, mentioning finding the room with the well in the garage.

"Can you talk about what happened with Dad?" he asked, quietly.

Regina looked at Harry, knowing the time had come for her to share the horror of her past.

Searching her memories, she retold the story she would rather forget than rehash again, especially with her children.

"It was a Thursday night, and Mike was working under the

Fastback. You know he loved that car, like he loved you boys." A tear crept into her eye, but she continued, visibly struggling. "We hadn't long moved into this house when Mike found the well in the back room, mostly hidden by shelves. He pulled the bucket up with the lamp but was afraid to unlock it."

Gradually tears began to fall.

"Mike was a smart guy. He knew things weren't 'normal' and the lamp could change things for the better—or for worse. He chose to leave the lamp and anything it contained."

"After…" she stammered, her composure failing whilst desperately trying to keep it together. "Afterwards…" she cried, her eyes now red and lips trembling. "The police came and said coyotes attacked him, but it didn't make sense. Coyotes attacking in town? And someone in a garage under a car? His body was decimated, nothing like what an animal would do. Decimated, but not consumed." She sobbed.

"But the police wouldn't be deterred?" Harry asked.

"They said he asked for it, leaving the garage door open while he worked under the car." His mother choked.

There was not a sound. Everyone held their breath as the story unfolded.

"I heard Mike. I heard those 'things' and I knew they were not coyotes. But no one would listen. After the inquest, I had the well bricked up…"

Harry took a deep breath, knowing what was coming.

"…to protect you boys," Regina finished.

The air in the room was thick enough to cut with a sharp knife: anguish, anger, empathy, fear, grief, horror, vengeance. Simple emotive words, alphabetical even, but the emotions they left were like the tightening fibers of ropes strangling their hearts, suffocating them.

Later, in the rear room of the garage, the air seemed to have warmed back to a more normal eighty degrees. They continued their talk of the out-worlds, the enemy, and about ideas to defeat them. Harry sat with Stacey on one side, Sam on the other with Beth beside him, all on camp chairs except Wazeem who took the stool, completing the circle.

"What drives the Grimole?" Stacey asked Wazeem. "I mean, is it just violence? Hunger? Revenge?"

"They serve Masters, Mistress Stacey," Wazeem replied thoughtfully. "There are two Grimole that hold a higher rank: Remus and Ludwig. They are more powerful and aware, and in turn, serve Rubezahl, the lead Grimole. He holds ultimate strength and capability."

"And what drives this Rubezahl?" Harry asked. The words *aware* and *capability* held special emphasis, and that wasn't lost on him.

"Power," Wazeem stated. "He creates an army to conquer all that exist."

Sam, who was shuffling some cards, looked over at Harry

who had his hands together, fingers touching but palms apart making a ball. They looked red hot, like from the heat of an ember, and then they were on fire!

"Dude, your hands!" he yelled.

Harry looked down at his hands, holding a flaming ball like a miniature meteorite. He pulled them apart, and the ball of fire grew as his hands separated. Closing them, the fireball decreased in unison until he clasped his hands together and it was gone.

"Dude," was all Sam could say, and then he looked down at his own hands which were shuffling the cards at such a speed they were starting to smoke, smelling of burning paper.

"Wow yourself, dude," Harry said with a wide grin.

"So, is this the start of your Blackjack casino career, Sam?" Beth asked. "Because it looks like you're going to need a new pack of cards, LOL."

"And so it is," Wazeem said like he expected nothing different. "You shall all have to learn to control these gifts. They will expand and you must evolve along with them."

Beth noticed a twinkling to the right of her in time to see Stacey completely translucent, disappearing before her eyes.

"Stacey, you're invisible!" she shouted, her pitch deepening with more than a hint of worry.

"No, not invisible," Stacey replied from her left, no longer transparent. "I just moved by thinking about it!" She returned to her seat, nervous but excited.

Beth thought about that a second. Had Stacey teleported?

That made her think about what the gift of time meant and then noticed that no one in the room was speaking.

In fact, they weren't moving. Not at all! It was like time had stopped.

She got up, went around the back of first Wazeem, then Stacey and Harry to Sam. She took a piece of chalk off the bench and drew a fake mustache on Sam's upper lip. Going back to sit down, she looked up to see Wazeem had a puzzled look on his face.

Maybe time did not stop for the Ancient One?

With the simplicity of a thought, time resumed, and things returned to normal.

Harry and Stacey saw the drawing on Sam's upper lip and giggled.

"What?" Sam knew something was going on.

"Yeah, that is so out there," Stacey said, as Harry showed Beth's artistry to him, using his phone camera.

*Oh, this is so wild,* Beth thought as her arm changed into Mjolnir, Thor's enchanted Hammer and then back again.

*Super cool,* Harry thought as he renewed his little trick with his hands, but this time with water.

Sam stood up, ran outside and to the garden where he picked one of Regina's red roses and raced inside, putting it on Beth's lap before returning to his seat, all in a millisecond and without anyone seeing him.

*You're the man,* he thought as he watched Beth look at the

flower, and then up and around the room in wonder. Then they locked eyes, and Sam winked with a boyish grin.

Wazeem looked on, his eyebrows raised, almost smiling at their horseplay.

THE REST OF THE DAY WAS SPENT TALKING ABOUT WHAT HAD been done throughout the ages on other worlds and what was coming, all the while practicing their new skills in smaller, more subtle ways.

They learned that the Grimole had been a parasite, ravishing world after world, their dreaded Borgil leading countless Grimole.

"What can we do to stop them?" Stacey asked. "To keep them out?"

"I'm afraid the time for that has come and gone, Mistress," Wazeem replied. "The door has been opened, and if it wasn't the well, they would have found another way in. I fear that there is even another way open to them already—a gateway that allows them to travel from world to world."

Harry recalled the earlier mention of the Lygard. "What of the Lygard? What can they do to help us?"

Wazeem looked down and cited the origin of the pride of the Perie. "The Perie are the trusted companions of the Su-dah! They behold the way with the Lygard. Only the Perie have that authority."

"Can you make contact with the Perie?" Stacey asked.

"Yes, Mistress Stacey," was the reply. "The Perie have always answered the call of the Arhmeic."

"Would you do that for us, Wazeem?" Stacey asked.

"Yes, Wazeem, would you please call them to help us?" Beth asked.

Wazeem reflected on memories of previous battles, supporting other worlds, and the brothers and sisters he fought with, both the living and the dead. Of the innocent slaughtered and the children orphaned by the Grimole invaders. More than help these young ones, he would fight for them. For humanity.

His agreement was met by hugs from the girls, surprising him but stirring an emotion long forgotten.

Affection, maybe?

THAT EVENING, ON THE OUTER SIDE OF MORNINGTON, BETH'S kid brother Stevie and his best friend Darryl Maddison had been to the local diner for an afternoon snack. Engrossed in video games, they got distracted, and the hour grew late.

Seeing it was after 6.30, Stevie said, "We've gotta split, bro."

They stepped outside to a deepening twilight, almost an hour later than they should have been leaving.

"My mom is going to freak," Stevie said.

"Yeah, well my dad's gonna be gunning for me," Darryl replied.

They grabbed their bikes and pedaled off for home, mindful of the few cars as the gaps between the streetlights grew and the shadows lengthened without the light of a moon.

"Oh crap, who's up there?" Darryl saw a couple of people ahead with pushbikes astride.

"Slow down, let's hang back a little," Stevie suggested, clearing his throat as his pitch changed.

They kept to the curb, undercover of the shadows of the overhanging trees while keeping a watchful eye on the figures ahead.

Caution was surely warranted as they realized that it was Brad Ogilvie and his quarterback Butch Rapsey, Rosedale High football stars, and renowned bullies directly ahead.

"Let's move onto the footpath and out-flank them," Stevie said. They had both been at the wrong end of confrontation with seniors at school and didn't want to go there again.

Darryl started to reply when there was a blood curdling wail from the darkness beyond.

"That's… really… close," Stevie whispered. His breath shuddered and the veins in his neck pulsated.

Darryl's eyes bulged unblinking, as the wailing escalated into a frenzy of shrieking.

His mouth dry, Stevie felt his heart pumping hard like it was going to explode, as they watched shapes like dogs appear from mid-air above Brad and Butch, circling them like birds of prey over carrions in the desert.

Before there was time to even think about it, the swirling

canines charged Butch from above, attacking him over and over as he screamed in terror. Brad backed into the shadows, whimpering as he watched on in shock.

"Time to go!" Stevie yelled to Darryl.

He grabbed his bike and started pedaling, leaving Darryl racing furiously to keep up. They reached Brad in moments and Stevie grabbed his arm, shaking him desperately.

"Come with us now!" he hollered as Butch was dragged off into the darkness, screaming and crying inhumanly.

Brad didn't need any more encouragement, and they raced up the street, hearts pounding and breath gasping. Leaving the unbelievable nightmare behind, the three of them looked at each other in disbelief.

Darryl reached out and touched Stevie's arm, stuttering, "What, uh, wh, what- wer-were they?" he managed to stammer.

Brad didn't say anything, his eyes blank, swaying backwards and forwards, not comprehending what he had just witnessed.

Stevie rubbed his forehead and shook his head. "We need to go home, like right now!" he half shouted, half cried.

TUESDAY DAWNED SUNNY, BUT A LITTLE COOLER AFTER OVERnight showers when Harry met Sam outside their bathroom and almost fell over in astonishment.

"What the heck happened to you?" Harry asked.

Sam looked back in equal awe. "What's got into you, Dude?

I don't have another painted mustache, do I? Or one eyebrow shaved or something?"

"Uh no, Bro, but you might want to take a look in the mirror."

Sam entered the bathroom, and the reflection silenced him with a gasp. He looked like he had added 20 pounds overnight— in muscle!

"Um, Dude, how am I gonna explain this?" Sam looked like he'd just had a PT push him on a totally protein three-month workout. "OMG, I'm freakin' buff!"

Harry tried to downplay it but wondered how they were going to keep this between them.

*Thank goodness school has finished for summer break,* Harry thought. They would have to be careful about this exposure and Sam's somewhat more pumped nature.

"Let's look if there's an old shirt of Dad's in the wardrobe," he said.

"Yeah, I won't be able to fight the girls off otherwise." Sam laughed. Flexing his newly acquired muscle, he showed his inner warrior.

Not so much Stacey and Beth. They kidded around, but were careful how they went about it, for the relationship between Harry and Stacey was cemented by years of trust, and she would never jeopardize the gain of the past few days.

Beth floated that Sam may have been taking something or had a Krypton spaceship hiding in the cornfields outside Smallville, with a wry grin.

"Ha, the only drug this body does is love, babe," Sam said with a grin.

"Settle down there, big fella," she replied, giving him a wink and a nod of approval.

# Chapter 6

Wednesday morning, the five of them met in the room off the garage again. It was another clear blue-sky day that was warming up at just eight o'clock, suggesting a hot summer to come.

But the warmth of the day disappeared, drawing cold with the mood as Beth recounted her brother Stevie's encounter to the others.

"So, they just appeared from nowhere and attacked," Harry stated. Trying to remain calm, he knew that this was a leap forward as the Borgil had breached their world. They had found a door that was not the well, and they would now keep coming.

"There's no time to waste. We have to make a plan—a plan to take these things down and protect everyone!" He was feeling some anger now and his hands started to warm—heating, glowing and burning, and then creating that small ball of fire that scared him, but excited him also.

"Can you tell us more about the Perie please, Wazeem?" Stacey asked. "Are they like handlers of the Lygard?"

Wazeem tried to explain over two thousand years of history in a matter of minutes.

"The Su-dah has won great battles throughout the ages, Mistress Stacey. We have beaten the Grimole before, but of late we have suffered only defeats." His voice wilted as he lost himself in the past. "Losses outweigh our victories. Valeo was our last, more than two hundred Earth years gone."

Clearly emotional, he continued. "Throughout time there have only been two constants: the Su-dah and the Lygard, who were gifted to the Perie after our first victory on their home world. But now there are no more Arhmeic, and the league of Su-dah runs dry while the Grimole only become stronger as their numbers increase, outnumbering us."

He paused briefly, before continuing, his speed and volume increasing in sync.

"The Perie are also no longer so many. Their strength is the Lygard, but so many fall as their first line of defense. They have been with us from almost the beginning, but I feel their ability to help could be coming to an end, as is that of the Su-dah." He finished with what could only be remorse, reflecting on defeat, foreseeing it even.

"Not yet." Harry stood bold and assertive. "We have abilities beyond other humans now, but from what you say about the Grimole, we will need all the help we can get."

"Yes, Wazeem," Stacey put her hand on his arm, looking him in the eyes. "We need your help, along with that of all of your allies so that we can defeat this common enemy."

Wazeem seemed genuinely inspired by their words. He had known many fierce warriors and even magical beings, but these humans seemed different somehow. He didn't understand it, but he knew to trust his Su-dah instincts.

Inspired, he elaborated. "The Perie are betrothed to the philosophies of nature, sisterhood, and faith. They live in a world that they must protect, whilst sharing an obligation to protect other worlds and fend off this common enemy that would obliterate them. Also, they believe in the Gods, in each other, and that there is a greater good for all. I will call the Perie to bring their Lygard, but I cannot know as to what their numbers might be, Mistress."

"That will be enough, thank you, Wazeem," Stacey replied. "Would you also do me another favor, though please?" she asked him carefully, not wanting to push things too far.

"Anything, Mistress Stacey." Wazeem seemed quite taken with the human—not that she would make an unreasonable request, of course.

"Would you please also tell us of all the other surviving worlds? You mention them, but we don't know who has stood and who has fallen. If there are worlds that would support us in our hour of need, it makes sense to reach out now." Her voice dwindled away.

"You are right again, Mistress Stacey," Wazeem replied.

Harry's shoulders pushed back with his chest puffed out, filled with pride at his girl.

"Romala fell, as did Olympia, Naga, and more. Perie, Xanthus, Valeo, Ladon, and Urania survived. Urania houses the Ancient Ones, and one of them refers to another world unknown—a world also in need like yours now, but one filled with fierce fighters that could help turn this tide for you. These worlds all have strength like I see in you. I will call to them, but the Grimole are growing stronger all the while. I suggest you bond with all these that you meet."

"Yes, Wazeem," Stacey said. "We need them all, and we need them now."

"One more thing, Wazeem," Harry interjected. "When you mentioned Remus and Ludwig, you said they were more aware. What did you mean? And Rubezahl's capability—what of that?"

"Well, that would be two things, Master Harry." Wazeem relaxed a little with what was the closest to a smile yet. "But I shall answer them both. Remus and Ludwig assist with the 'production' of Grimole, for they are animal, but not born of nature; they are bred and for a single purpose only: to serve and conquer. They are born alongside their ungodly hounds, the Borgil. Rubezahl controls them all with an ability that has conquered many worlds. He has taken many from us and only six that we know of now remain."

"Six is enough." Stacey was emphatic. "We have the Perie and the Lygard. We have us!"

At first Harry wondered where everyone would go, but Wazeem had already accounted for this: the room off the garage with the well now housed seven doors, one for each world, with a name burned into a hardwood sign above the first five.

"Umm, just not sure how this is going to help, Dude," Sam said.

Wazeem opened the first door, with the name Ladon above. Inside was a sixteen-foot-wide corridor with seven more imposing doors. Wazeem opened the closest, most prestigious door and beyond lay the most enormous hall. There were only about eight hundred Ladonians inside but there was enough room for four times as many! There were other doors leading off, several large open kitchens, chairs and tables, bars, fireplaces and entertainment areas.

"Through these other doors are bathrooms, guest quarters, gymnasiums, swimming pools, meditation/prayer rooms and gardens," Wazeem explained. "The other doors from the main corridor have similar facilities, some with stables, training facilities, archery ranges and almost anything else required."

"Stables?" Stacey asked.

"Yes, Mistress Stacey," he responded, as formal as ever, "for horses. There are also some that have areas for catapult training."

"How big of areas?"

"No less than 10 square miles."

"But where is all of this? Not in our garage, for sure." Sam was a little lost.

"Well, Wazeem didn't just squeeze into the lamp, did he?" Harry prompted, smiling.

"No, Master Harry. Indeed, I had all the room in the world," the off-worlder finished, this time managing his first full smile.

"So, five doors for five worlds, and a sixth for the garage, but where does the seventh door lead?"

"That door is where we will stand our ground, Master Harry," he replied quietly, his heart heavy and his gaze dropping.

"You mean we will fight the battle in there?" Stacey was shocked. "In a room off the Porter's garage?"

"I think this is all getting very loco, if you know what I mean." Sam pointed to his head with his right index finger completing clockwise circles while rolling his eyes, trying to lighten the mood.

"That door leads not to a room, Master Sam, but to a place like Earth. A dimension of Earth where we must win this battle."

"Must win," Stacey replied, not missing much. "Are there going to be that many of them?"

"An army made with the sole purpose of annihilating worlds, yes, Mistress Stacey. There will be as many as we can muster times twenty. We must be capable, and we must be aware, for there is no tomorrow for mankind unless we win this day. The battle must be won here on Earth. United, we must win at all costs!"

His reply was not lost on any of them.

"Then we will need every able body, to hone our skills, and grab whatever advantage we can find to take them down!" Stacey almost shouted.

"Indeed, Mistress. Tomorrow you shall be formally introduced to the Xanthu, by Perie royalty."

LATER THAT NIGHT, LYING IN BED AS THE INKY DARKNESS OF the night slipped over them, Harry thought he heard a noise. He opened his eyes, feeling uneasy, like something was wrong.

From the blackness, dog-like shapes appeared: two, three, four—he could barely count them as they circled above him, floating, flying around and around snarling, growling, wild-eyed and seething with rage. He couldn't define their forms exactly as they swirled together almost as one, howling like rabid wolves with menacing jaws housing drooling canines, and their yellow eyes piercing the darkness. The faster the shapes swirled, the more they became conjoined, almost animated and merging then disappearing, until they were gone altogether.

His eyes still adjusting to the dark, Harry saw a figure emerge: a humanoid figure on two feet, but half crouched over, barely four and a quarter foot tall. Red and black, its bald triangular head with large, pointed ears stood before him, a creature of an ungodly world. It had a large nose with a ruddy tip that also surrounded luminous green eyes and matched pursed red lips that lead to a pointed chin. The body was spiny, but the arms and legs, feet and hands were disproportionately large. Dressed in hessian pants held up by a green sash, leather bands encircled both upper arms with a matching necklace, all embellished with long pointed teeth, trophies from some past conquest.

"Ha-ha, the puny human thinks it can beat us." The throaty voice came from the darkness. It was self-assured and positively hideous.

Ludwig did not need any introduction with the letters tattooed L-U-D on three fingers below the knuckle on the left hand and W-I-G mirrored on the right.

*Half of each thumb is missing,* Harry thought. *How odd.*

"It thinks…" the gravelly voice repeated. "It thinks it can beat us." It squealed an inhuman gurgle as its lips peeled back exposing deadly teeth. "It thinks it can beat us," he scratched out again.

"I don't think. I know!" Harry said, balling up his fists.

"Die, human dog!" The Goblin brought his sword at Harry and leaned in to pierce his midriff.

"Sam! Sam! The enemy is upon us! Sam!" Harry yelled, gasping as he struggled to catch his breath and clenching his eyes shut.

OPENING HIS EYES, HIS HEART POUNDING AND BREATH GASP-
ing, Harry realized it had just been a dream.

He was still shaking when a blood-curdling howl came from
the street below, followed by more hyena-like yowling and the
terrifying screams of what could only be people under attack.
Unsure if he was awake after all, he felt cloudy and half-dazed.
The cries continued, jolting him like an electric shock. Leaping
out of bed and looking out the window, he saw his dream unfold
in the street below.

This was reality for sure but mixed with the supernatural
as dog-like shapes besieged people, ravishing them under the
streetlamp. As he watched, the shapes became more dog-like as
the creatures pounced on one of his neighbors.

A man with a shovel tried to fight them off but for every
one that he defended against, another appeared from above or
behind, always circling and savaging flesh with razor sharp jaws
and claws, tearing them apart piece by piece before moving onto
another, hungry for the kill.

Harry charged down the stairs and outside, dressed only
in his pajamas with his fists opening and closing. His fingers
flexed as his hands warmed, glowing orange and becoming nova
red-hot.

One of the shapes came close enough to touch him, but its
howl was cut off as it perished instantly. Ablaze at 300 degrees, his

ability cooked it instantly, and it lay smoldering on the sidewalk.

Not an animal to pity, this was an evil abomination—a machine manufactured to kill—and so he felt no emotion. The smell of death and burning flesh filled the air as he incinerated another with fire and flame. Then Sam appeared in a blur, striking them down, and two more lay dead at his feet.

"So, you heard the ruckus?" Harry asked.

"No, you called, right?" Sam said. "I heard you call me. I was asleep and then I heard you calling my name."

"No, I just thought it," Harry said aloud but wondered about that.

Could their brotherly bond support unspoken communication?

Or was that stretching science fiction?

Harry cremated three of the four bodies of the dogs. The fourth Borgil they took to the garage workbench to get a closer look. It was one that Sam had killed with his bare hands, so it was still intact for examination.

"Behold the weapon of the enemy." Wazeem had slipped in quietly behind them.

"Jeepers, dude. Don't do that!" Sam thought he was going to have a heart attack!

On the bench lay the Borgil, a canine of types. It had a silky coat that was of neither cat nor dog. It was of the deepest black tinged with blue that was more like skin than fur. It had four legs like a dog, but each one had four digits that were almost like the talons of an eagle and the sharpest pointed claws. The elongated snout was equipped with equally sharp teeth and its muscular body had no fat. All of its ribs were visible. The eyes were like the blackest marbles in a sickly yellow cesspool, and its ears were unduly long. Even dead, danger emanated off the thing.

"If this is their pet, I can't wait to meet the owner," Sam said.

His modern sarcasm was lost on Wazeem. "Oh, you will meet them, Master Sam. They are simply sending the Borgil to test our resolve."

"Reconnaissance missions, yeah, I get that. And what should we expect when we meet this enemy?" Harry asked. He needed to understand what they were up against.

Wazeem did not reply immediately. When he did, he spoke quietly and carefully. "The Grimole and their dogs, is perhaps a topic best shared with Mistresses Stacey and Bethany before any meeting takes them unaware, don't you think, Master Harry?"

Returning to bed, the night was black with no moon, but the temperature was mild, and there was a light breeze heading into an early summer. Eventually the boys returned to sleep.

Sam had the window open, and the curtains fluttered lightly when a shadow crossed the floor, up the wall, and onto the ceiling.

He woke up knowing there was a presence in the room: it was a movement that he could feel from the vibrations in his body. Opening his eyes, he saw a shadow on the wall—the shadow of a person.

The figure was joined by a figure of a dog, snarling with bared teeth. And then there was a second one, another Borgil, and then a third!

*Harry!* Sam thought instinctively. With supersonic speed, he smashed one of the dogs with an iron fist, and then another, and immediately a third.

With three hounds lying at his feet, Sam stood face to face with another demon: a figure of about five-and-a-half-feet tall wearing a dirty, dark blue cloak with a hood that allowed his elongated ears to protrude. The creature's eyes were white, but bloodshot with green veins from luminous green irises, matched by a green sash circling ragged pants and brown leather sandals that strapped bony legs to the knees.

With wrinkled sagging skin it stared at Sam, not saying a word, just scowling intently and even more menacing.

"Sam!" a voice came to him through the fog. "Sam!"

Sam jolted awake—it was just a dream!

*No way,* he thought, but the room was empty.

He lay there thinking about what had just happened when Harry appeared beside him.

"Sam," he said. "What's wrong?"

Sheepishly Sam blew him off. "Nothing, why?"

"You called me." Harry was confused. *What the…?*

Sam continued to downplay it and eventually Harry gave up, returning to bed.

Sam didn't understand it either, but he was too embarrassed to think that this could have just been a bad dream. And to have called out to Harry like that…

*But I didn't call him…* was his last thought, before drifting back to sleep.

Lying in his own bed, Harry wondered about the way that they had reached out to each other. Their bond had evolved, telepathically even.

THE NEXT MORNING, AS THEY WERE BEING ESCORTED TO MEET the Perie, they passed the open door of Ladon, where four Ladonians greeted them.

Wazeem introduced Kurkri, their Chieftain, Sheelah, his wife, and their sons, Minor and Tross.

Kurkri was a massive man with arms bigger than most men's waists. He was around seven feet tall and nearly three in girth. With heavily tattooed arms, bearded, and with long plaited hair, he wore leather, cloth and fur, resembling a Viking of old.

His wife was not quite as tall, though still physically domineering, but their sons were even bigger at nearly eight feet. Their weapons were dagger, sword, and shield, but there were spears, helmets, and cudgels resting on the floor around them.

In spite of their enormous size and intimidating appearance,

Kurkri and Sheehlah's greetings were very welcoming. Their sons, Minor and Tross, towered above them, drinking beer from one liter steins that looked like teacups in their massive hands.

"You are well equipped, little ones, but are you up to the fight?" Tross challenged, with a menacing tone, beer dripping down his beard.

"We can hold our own," Harry replied.

"Yes, but does that mean you will kill the dogs? And their goblin masters? You will fight and shed blood, dying beside us?" Tross asked.

"Have we seen the enemy?" Sam returned, holding his stony gaze. "Yes, we have seen them! We have seen the enemy that controls the dog, the one that has helped conquer many worlds of late; for he looked into my eyes just last night. He told me that he would now take Earth, and that Ladon would fall along with us. But the devil chose not to fight me then. Is that your wish now?"

A silence fell upon them as everyone held their breath.

Minor put his hand on Tross' arm.

"My brother has had too much to drink, Master Sam. He respects you and apologizes."

"Yes, Minor, we mean no disrespect to you," Stacey replied, now also playing the diplomat. "We appreciate your presence and welcome you here."

"We hold true to the allegiance." Sam felt a little awkward for having been so hostile, but the weight of his dream stayed fresh in his mind.

As they made to move on, Stacey asked Kurkri how many Ladonians would be here to help them fight.

"Indeed, we have over four thousand and expect as least four times as many more to join us in the coming days."

*So more than sixteen thousand,* Stacey thought. She thanked him, wondering if that would be enough as they made to move on.

Meanwhile, Harry was deep in thought, contemplating what Sam had said: that the enemy he had seen was the one that controlled the dog and he looked into his eyes last night.

THE OVERHEAD SIGN ON THE 2ND DOOR SIMPLY READ "PERIE," but Harry knew this would be anything but simple as they entered the hall to see a room of sixty by three hundred feet, with a single kitchen, six doors that led to bathrooms, sleeping quarters, and the like. There were only about ninety of the female warriors in the room, but some hundred and eighty Lygard lay at their feet—canines of legend, content to be near their mistresses.

Moving forward to meet their Perie welcoming party first was Sari, warrior Queen, with Aquiel, her sister and leading Council, and lastly Issy, the Queen's adolescent daughter.

"We are honored to meet you, Your Highness." Stacey curtseyed.

"Yes, honored, Your Majesty." Beth followed suit. "Aren't we, Samuel?"

Sam could not resist. "Honored indeed, m'lady, to be sure, to be sure," he said in his best Irish leprechaun accent.

*OH GOD,* Harry thought, but merely muttered, "Your Highness," while trying not to smile.

Not dissimilar in size or statute to humans, the Perie were well versed with English and with the ways of the world.

"We've been watching you for some time," Sari said. At just over five and a half feet, she was hardly tall but commanded her presence over them all. With blonde hair and blue eyes, she had a bronzed complexion and wore clothes of leather with a Lycra blend with gold plates. She could've been a cross between the Amazon heroines of old and the futuristic women from *Star Trek.*

"And even walking amongst us, at times?" Harry asked tentatively.

"Well, that may be so, Master Harry," Sari replied.

"Just Harry will be fine, thanks, Your Highness." He grinned.

"And simply Sari from you also, Harry." She smiled in return.

Aquiel was equally beautiful, but oppositely dark haired, fair skinned, and brown eyed. Wearing more of the new-age Lycra, also sporting bracelets of gold, like her sister, she held a serious responsibility to the people she helped govern.

Issy, however, was a little more modern. A mixture of Sari and her aunt, she had brunette hair, green eyes and lightly golden skin. She had an attitude that said she was the Queen's daughter, and that you had better not forget it.

There was a small entourage of soldiers, but they had no

armor and carried only swords. When asked about the lack of protection, their queen shouted, "Manica!"

Shields appeared like magic, covering them in interlocking layers that clicked outwards, overlapping like that of an ancient dinosaur.

"Manica—that's an ancient Latin word for sleeve, isn't it?" Harry asked. "It was metal plates fastened together by leather used as protection in battle." He wondered how a Latin word became integrated into an off-world culture light years ahead in sophistication.

"You are very astute, Harry," Sari replied, looking at Wazeem. "Quite the student, I'm sure."

She then addressed their great hall. "My Sisters, I bring to you our new partners in this endeavor: Harry, Stacey, Sam, and Bethany, who swear an oath of fealty. We, in turn, swear homage to the world of man and to free the last of the known worlds. With our Lygard we will take lead, supported by their armies, for Earth is the new battleground, and this will be the final chapter in our fight against the old enemy! Our off-world allies will also send everyone they can this one last time. There is no retreat, no surrender, and a loss is not conceivable. We must be victorious!"

The room erupted with a cheer with bellows of "Hail Sari" and "Hail Aquiel."

"Perie—is that an adaptation of where the Persian mythology Peri came from?" Harry asked. "An evil but subsequently good genie or fairy?"

A five-foot eight-inch woman with flaming red hair and brilliant green eyes strode forth and addressed him. "I am Tyla, cousin to Sari and Aquiel. We know of this folklore to which you refer."

"Do you think the Persians might've based this legend on yourselves?" Harry asked boldly.

Stacey elbowed him, wondering where this was going.

"Well, I'm not sure, but we are no genies," Tyla replied with a laugh.

"Neither genie nor evil, my lady." Harry was leading to something. "But graceful indeed, and fairies are renowned for two things: their craft and enchanting voices. Would you indulge us in one or the other, fair Tyla?"

Tyla gave a slight blush and then started to sing in a perfect pitch, unaccompanied by music. Soon another and then another joined her in harmony with words of a language not known to their guests. Then a lyre, an old harp-like instrument, joined in, as even more voices harmonized.

"Perie is a Persian name, but the Greeks had another: Sirens. Your song is so remarkable it could be attributed to the mythology of both, Tyla. It's truly magical," Harry said.

A flush swept across Tyla's cheeks, and she cleared her throat, thanking him.

Stacey was stunned. Sam and Beth both looked at each other in amazement. Harry's knowledge was extraordinary. It was almost as if he could read people and knew the right things to say.

The humming dwindled off, and Tyla addressed Harry. "The Sisterhood of the Perie welcomes our new brothers and sisters. We are honored to fight alongside you!"

The Perie shared their defenses: formation working together, and ultimately the Manica, something the boys were excited to learn about, for it was truly so astounding. It turned out to be a lot more than a simple shoulder shield, able to cover arms or legs or any part of the body, individually or combined. It was robotic as the golden plates extended and retracted from various limbs, head, and torso like those from a science fiction movie.

Then the Perie showed their offenses. Swords, spears, knives, and daggers they knew, but these advanced warriors had a weapon so far undisclosed. "It is the way of the voice," Issy instructed, issuing earplugs.

*Sirens indeed,* Harry thought.

The Queen's sister then showed them the technique: she held her hand up and directed her voice forward, building in pitch until a vibration emitted with sound.

*Perfect sonics,* Harry thought, astounded.

*Holy cow,* Sam thought.

She continued to increase in volume and in pitch until a plate smashed and a glass shattered under the force of her sound.

This was a weapon with incredible power—sound that could destroy solid objects.

*But could it be replicated?* Stacey wondered. Looking up, she saw Harry staring at her, reflecting what she was thinking with a knowing look that no longer surprised her.

Then it was the human's turn to show their talent. Harry started by cupping his hands, which started to glow warmly, and a small spark once again became a glowing ball. The Perie looked on with wonder as it increased, becoming larger. Even the other teens were amazed when he held his arms wide apart with a blazing inferno over three feet wide. He slowly pulled his hands together, and it reduced in size and intensity to match, until it was merely the size of his hand. Then a wave extinguished the flames, and Harry was left handling half a gallon of swirling crystal blue water. Slowly he closed his hands, and the water diminished to the sounds of wonder and admiration amongst the room.

Around the Perie hall there were 80 candelabras, spaced approximately nine feet apart and mounted off the wall just over head height. Sam stood up and in supersonic speed raced around the room, lighting every second one before returning to his seat. In a moment, everyone could see what had happened, as if he had flicked a light switch. The Perie gasped in surprise, but not yet done, Sam repeated the act with every other candle that had not been lit on the first round. The Perie cheered and Sam repeated his round yet again, but this time extinguishing all the torches in one lightning second before they had finished clapping. It was quite a show!

Not to be outdone, Beth stopped time. She got up from her seat, looking around the room at everyone motionless, like mannequins in a store window. At a leisurely pace, she grabbed a long pole wrapped with an oiled cloth and proceeded to light every second candle that Sam had first lit. About a third of the way through, she caught movement out of the corner of her eye and turned to see Harry lighting one. He was not frozen!

"So, you can slip out of my time zone?" she asked. Beth felt a little jealous that this was not just her thing and hers alone, but she was not the petty type. Her cheeks flushed, but rather than show any sullen childishness, she opened her mind to the reality of Harry sharing her newfound power.

"Yeah, it seems I am acquiring new skills whether I would want them or not. But I'd like to hope that there is a purpose to what we are all experiencing, and that the expansion of my abilities aides the cause."

"Abilities? So more than just this?"

"Yes, Beth, more than one," he confirmed.

They finished the lighting and sat down, but then Beth jumped up again and went to Sam, pulling something from her pocket. It was a lipstick which she used to draw a small bubble-gum pink kiss on his cheek, smiling at Harry as she returned to her seat. Time resumed, and the room gasped, amazed and equally bemused by what she had done. Gasps of wonder turned to cheers of applause and laughter as the Perie realized that something truly special was happening.

Sam flushed red, and Issy, sitting beside him, showed her displeasure, helping him wipe the kiss off with a tissue.

Beth then paused time once more, extinguished the candles with Harry assisting from the onset this time, and then completed the show with a second set of bright candy pink lips, this time on Sam's other cheek. Resuming normal time, everyone laughed, with the exception of Issy.

Harry looked at Beth, who returned a knowing smile. He knew she had feelings for Sam, but it had taken the threat of Issy to motivate her.

Lastly, Beth exhibited her ability to change form, imitating the Hulk's massive green arm with bulging biceps and forearm, and then changing to a sword of the Samurai and lastly an arm made of orange rocks like Thing from the comics of *The Fantastic Four*. The room cheered loudly and clapped together like the crowds of Roman arenas celebrating the gladiators of old until her arm returned to normal—well all clapped except for Issy.

Next, it was Stacey's turn. She stood up and started by disappearing before reappearing and then repeating it several times. Concentrating, she willed the candle lighter to rise and ignite all of the candles that Beth had just doused.

"Telekinesis!" Beth shouted over the clapping and accolades. "You never told us about that!"

"Well, it's kind of just developing," she said, a little abashed. "Want to have a go?" Stacey asked Harry, suspecting his abilities also included this.

"Sure," he replied, rising and smothering the flames Stacey had lit just by thinking about it. Then he looked at Stacey, and every single candle in the room burst into flame simultaneously.

"So, you have it now, too." She already knew the answer without needing to ask the question.

"Yeah, seems like I'm being inundated with tricks," he joked, though there was an underlying note of concern in his voice.

The Perie, unaware of this, celebrated their new friends and their abilities, feasting and toasting.

"Will you tell us more of the Lygard?" Stacey asked Tyla a little later, giving one of their companions a belly rub.

"The Lygard are considered gifts from the Gods," the royal replied. "They have been with the Perie since time began, forever loyal and willing to fight and die for us."

"Yes, but do you breed them, or do they breed themselves?"

"Oh, we have a very strict breeding program. They are all purebreds of set bloodlines. We do this to protect them."

"They are very smart, aren't they?"

Tyla nodded and smiled. "His name is Slade. He likes you. You have a way with him."

They were like a Siberian Husky, of the purist white, yet also equally black. But unlike a domestic Husky, the Lygard had triangular ears and a large wide snout. They also housed not one but two rows of incisors and canines similar to a shark with multiple rows of teeth. Their body was built for speed and strength with long muscular legs, and they were overall larger than a

Husky at a hundred and twenty pounds. And there was no gray or mixed color to their thick coat.

"He's just beautiful," Stacey said, looking at eyes that were pure white with black pupils and translucent irises. Apart from the varying patterns of their coats, the color of their iris was the only thing that differed amongst the canine cross lupine, with others being red, green, or yellow.

*Canine cross lupine,* she thought. *Canalupine.*

*Or Lucanine.* Harry's voice entered her mind.

She looked up and caught his look. Smiling, Stacey was now aware of his supernatural ability to join her telepathically.

"Do you know how many more Perie might join us, Tyla?" she asked tentatively.

"All who are able will come to join us," the Queen's sister replied. The two of them were forming a very close bond, quickly and naturally.

"We are but the royal party. Another eight thousand will come when they have prepared their Lygard." Now she paused, and Stacey could tell there was heaviness in her heart. "Twenty Lygard will join each of us to repel the Borgil."

"One hundred and sixty thousand!" Stacey was astounded at the number and overwhelmed at the implication of what Tyla was saying. She continued to rub her new friend's midriff, who lay grunting with pleasure, both of them loving every moment of it, as she agonized over the thought of the vast number of Lygard and their potential for loss.

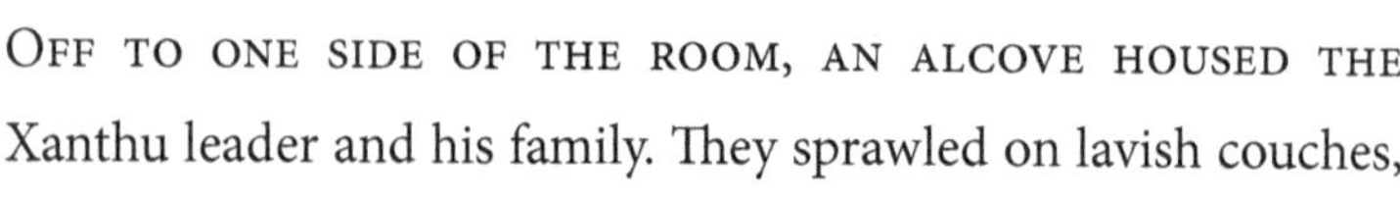

OFF TO ONE SIDE OF THE ROOM, AN ALCOVE HOUSED THE Xanthu leader and his family. They sprawled on lavish couches, fanned by servants with an array of jungle animals around them.

Jotun, their king, his wife Sakra, and their sons Nanda and Anu with their daughter Rahu enjoyed Perie hospitality.

"The Xanthu have great power." Sari introduced this new allegiance to them openly. "They harness the strength of the jungle and the animals that inhabit it."

"Power, Sari?" the King replied. "There is no power. We are but a simple people, just trying to get along with nature."

Harry suspected that he was downplaying that, with an underlying *something* that was yet to be seen.

But the Xanthu leader remained coy, reluctant to show these strangers anything, even if they were friends of friends.

Stacey was not having any of that. They needed every soul that they could muster, and the Xanthu had fought these demons before.

She greeted Jotun. "Your highness, My lord...," she started, unsure how to address him.

"Jotun is good enough for me." The reply was reserved, to say the least.

"Then maybe it will also be enough for friends, if I may be so bold," she presented.

"You may presume too much, young one."

*This was going to be hard work,* Stacey thought.

"Jotun, these are beautiful animals you have here." She gestured towards two lionesses at their feet, with two tigers on the left side and two leopards on the right.

"And…?"

He was really hard work!

"One of the leopards has trouble with its paw. I don't know if it's a break or something, but I could take a look if you want me to?"

"How can you know that, for you have just arrived and not seen her walk?" he asked, cocking his head in intrigue.

"I have a way, Jotun," she simply said, maintaining strong eye contact.

"You may look at the Pard, young one, but take care when you do, for a pained animal can also be a dangerous one."

"Pard—that's an ancient Greek word for leopard, derived from several languages: 'Leo' and 'Pard,' is that right?" Harry said.

*Harry is developing a habit of this,* Stacey thought.

"You know things, yes, young one." The Xanthu leader was unsure how Harry would know such detail. He then looked in wonder as Stacey greeted the leopard, gaining her trust with some crooning and inspecting her injured paw.

"Her name is Zalie, and she carries a poison thorn from your home world called the Tristle," she proclaimed. "It threatens her life."

"But how can you know any of this?" Nanda asked.

"Silence, son, let the cat speak!" his father demanded.

Stacey didn't know what that meant, but guessed if the leopard let her help, she was doing okay. She touched the creature's head, stroked her side, and slowly lifted the injured paw. Zalie groaned but allowed Stacey to gently work the thorn from between her pads. But removing the thorn was only the first stage. The poison still remained. Stacey looked at Harry, who knew what that meant—and what had to be done.

To heal the animal, Stacey had to extract the poison from the animal—and the pain along with it. The cost was enormous, with tentacles stretching like blue veins that extended throughout her body, trading her health for that of the one she was healing—this great cat. Stacey started to sway, her strength waning as her body paled, shaking as her skin pulsated.

Just as Harry was about to put a stop to it, it was over. The poison was gone and Stacey fell backwards, not unconscious, but clearly suffering.

After a few minutes, Stacey murmured as Zalie licked her, fully healed and seemingly aware of the human's assistance.

"Never has this happened before!" Jotun exclaimed. "You have the ways of the medicine. Only the Elders have ever done this before. You have the ability to heal the dying!"

His family knew that King Jotun was gifted with the ability to favor the spirits of generations before, but war had crippled their race these past times, stealing many tribes. They worried he would give his loyalty too easily to the wrong union one day, from someone who did not have Xanthu interests in their best interest.

But Harry knew what to say.

"Jotun, we know the cost of battle is high. We know that you have suffered heavy losses in previous encounters, but if we do not win this battle, there will be no tomorrow for Xanthus. You will be annihilated next if Earth, and those who side with us, cannot prevail. There is no sitting on the side, nor any siding with the enemy, for they neither want, nor need allies. I beg you, please join this fight and commit all who can to defend your home world. We have shown you something of the power of man, and we believe there is more power of the Xanthu. Would you join us?"

The aging king looked at his wife and children for support, considering what he had seen today against the losses of the past. Beth then imitated the great cats of the room, firstly with her arms becoming those of a tiger, then her front torso, head included, a leopard, and finally that of a lion.

The Xanthu were amazed but not to be outdone, Nanda and Anu's heads became those of tigers while Rahu resembled that of a panther.

"We don't become our jungle warriors," Jotun proclaimed as he and Sakra exhibited the facial features of a lion and lioness. "We merely request their help."

The Xanthu, it seemed, did much more than that. The animals connected with them.

"We do not become them," Rahu whispered to Stacey. "We join them."

"We'll look forward to seeing that," Stacey replied and took her arm.

They were led to a second door off the main Xanthus door to a replica jungle, where they were shown the incredible talents of the Xanthu.

Zalie greeted Stacey as if she had mothered her. The bond of healing could not be argued, nor could the well-being of the animal. Stacey reveled in the cat's affection.

They saw the warriors' heads metamorphosing to become that of elephants, and then there was a real herd with them, trumpeting and talking to each other. Some became the heads of bears: Black, Grizzly, and Kodiak, and then real bears appeared, growling in communication with the off-worlders.

More still took the appearance of gorillas, orangutans, and chimpanzees, and they also spoke but with grunts and laughing of *he, he, he.* Others were rhinos of both white and black, and of course the great cats: lions, tigers, leopards, cheetahs, pumas and panthers, all being assumed by the Xanthu and then joined by real rhinos and cats, becoming one together.

It was jungle power!

The bond of humans and Xanthu continued to grow, and when it was time to leave, Jotun offered their allegiance to join in the fight against the Grimole. Most importantly, his family supported their king, and his decision. The humans thanked him graciously, and Stacey politely asked how many he thought would be coming to support them.

"We are but ten thousand strong now, young one, and all will come with our jungle warriors to support us."

"That is most gracious of you, Jotun. You will be most welcome."

# Chapter 8

Next morning the boys met Stacey and Beth outside the garage, then went into the "Off-G room" as Sam called it (off-grid, he said, but Harry really thought off-gate was more accurate). There they met Wazeem.

"Things are going to be a little different today," he said in greeting. "We will be going further, doing and seeing much more, but I will be slowing things down. No cause for panic, just try to relax."

"And enjoy the ride! Tray tables folded and seats in an upright position. What's next, a magic carpet?" Sam joked.

"No, Master Sam, there is no magic carpet, I'm afraid." Wazeem looked at him, thinking this boy was maybe born upside down or dropped on his head even.

They entered the unmarked seventh door, where the most

beautiful green landscape lay before them, bathed in clear blue skies and brilliant sunshine.

"OMG this is so gorgeous!" Beth gasped. Heading off, about a quarter mile on, was a small, abandoned village where some soldiers had bedded down the night before. There, they found three black stallions and two white mares.

"But I don't know how to ride," Stacey said.

"Yes, you do now. You all do," Wazeem replied.

*Maybe this was one of the gifts Wazeem has given us,* Stacey thought.

Greeting their horses, they saddled up with help from soldiers from the Royal British mounted guard and headed into the valley beyond. Sure enough, they knew how to mount and ride.

After riding for a while, they came across another camp, this one from Japan—the mounted soldiers of the Samurai. They lunched with these new allies before heading further into the valley, when an object in the distance caught their attention.

"It's the Great Wall of China!" Stacey exclaimed. "But how can that be?"

"It's not that great wall, but a great wall nonetheless," Harry surmised.

"Correct, Master Harry," Wazeem confirmed. "It is a wall made for this battle, and this one only. Unlike the Great Wall of 13,000 miles built over some 2,500 years, this one was built this past year and is but thirty-five miles long. However, this one does have many features that the Great Wall doesn't."

"Like…?" Sam asked.

"Beacon towers, barriers, barracks, stables, armories, garrison stations, fortresses, catapults. It also has better protection given that it encircles a valley, whereas Genghis Khan and the Mongols easily exposed China's Great Wall's many weaknesses."

"Well, I don't know much about that, but I do know we wouldn't want any flaws in our wall." Sam had a knack for the obvious.

"Most of the materials of the Great Wall are just mud and only 500 years old. It is also several walls, not one, like people think, and the literal translation is Long Wall, not Great Wall," Harry finished.

"Yes, Dr. Einstein, great description."

Sam's reference confused Wazeem. "Master Sam, to whom do you refer to when you mention this Doctor Einstein? I did not know Master Harry was a man of medicine."

The teens looked at each other and laughed.

"Hey, Wazeem, that's okay. It's just Sam joking around. You have to learn to ignore his mediocre wit," Beth explained with a twinkle in her eye and a smiling sideways look at Sam who pretended offense but couldn't hold back a wry smile. "Maybe something slightly better than mediocre?" he asked.

"Maybe," she replied, giving him a wider grin now.

"Whoo-hoo!" he cheered and clicked his heels to spur his ride on, racing ahead.

When they reached the wall, they marveled at its

construction.

"Wow, this is amazing!" Stacey said.

"Impressive, for real," Harry concurred.

It was a wall of solid block, some 25 feet high, 18 feet deep and evenly constructed. There were battlements every mile with catapults. The walls were double-blocked, with beacon towers that could light the skies, and garrisons were placed at every second tower. Stables, armories, and barracks were stationed to house, arm, and protect those defending inside. Spanning some nine feet wide, it had room to move and act as a road, moving people, horses, and carts with equipment. They entered the wall by an impressive gate on the north side. Further up, the wall just ended, but construction was clearly not finished.

"Will it be ready in time?" Harry's wrinkled brow showed concern as he surveyed the wall that was to be their last line of defense.

"We are working as fast as we can, while slowing time," Wazeem replied. "Master Sam and Mistress Beth can help us with that."

Beth and Sam locked gazes, knowing that their newly acquired powers were the topic of conversation, potentially something to win wars and save worlds, even. They wondered as to their ability to make such a difference, and the burden that was being placed on them to get this job done.

Inside the wall, there were a lot of camps with many nations, and tens of thousands of men. Asia, Europe, the Americas,

Africa, and Oceania—all continents of Earth—had been called by the Su-dah to come together in a common cause to defend their world and the world of others, after thousands of years of warring among themselves.

"So many!" Stacey exclaimed.

"And different cultures," Harry agreed.

They made their way through the barracks of man, marveling at how they varied in custom but were united now. Thousands of them building the wall, using rocks they bolstered to block and brick, carried by horse and cart, with water and mortar carried by mule and dray. It was tiring, arduous work, but they took to it willingly, knowing their lives and those of so many more depended upon it.

They were now also starting to command those around them with their newly acquired abilities and rapid maturity. These four teenagers were quickly becoming leaders of man, and maybe even of worlds beyond.

As they made camp with Russians, Africans, Scots, Mexicans, and Native Americans, Harry thought, *A United Nations for real.*

"But how will we escape if need be?" Stacey asked. "There's no tunnel to get out!" Her throat tightened as she realized that if the enemy could not be stopped at the wall, they could only retreat upwards to try and hold the high ground. Women and children unable to fight would perish alongside their fighters and ultimately there would be no escape. The wall was their last line of defense. Stacey desperately tried to check her emotions, determined not to upset the mood.

Nobody said a word or even looked her in the eyes, but she was grateful when Harry grasped her hand, as a tear trickled down her cheek.

MEETING THE SCOTTISH REMINDED THEM OF THE LADONIANS— fierce warriors who met their enemy with sword and shield, but their friends with feast and ale.

"Scottish names," Sam slurred slightly while celebrating with their hosts, "are all Mac: MacPherson, MacDonald, and Macgregor. Why is that?"

Harry entered the conversation, always manner-of-fact. "That's because in Scottish history, the native language Mac means 'son of' so they were named the likes of son of Donald, son of Gregory."

"And in my case, my grandfather became son of Dougal, m'boy." A wild-looking Highlander of six-foot-eight stood before him. Lachlan McDougal had a head of red hair equally matched by a wild beard and mustache, and built like a giant, was every bit the clan leader. This Scotsman had taken quite a liking to the teens, especially Sam.

They talked warfare and love, Sam trying to act well beyond his years and Lachlan acting like he was younger again, much to the cheerful teasing of his wife, Morag. Her hair was equally red, and their similar looks matched more like they were siblings than husband and wife. Lachlan and Morag's daughter Bonnie also took quite a shine to Sam, something that was not lost on Beth. Bonnie had the same flaming red hair as her parents and was of a similar age to Sam, to whom she served food and ale, whether requested or not. Everyone enjoyed the moment, for humanity had long been divided, but was uniting now!

THAT NIGHT WAS THEIR SECOND TO LAST ON FIGHTWORLD, AS Sam called it. "Like Fighter-town," he had said, "and there is still our other world out there." And so, the name stuck.

With just the five of them surrounding a warm fire, Harry had more questions for Wazeem.

"Why do we only fight with outmoded weapons? We have more types of tanks than you could count, F15, F16, F22, F35 and probably five other F-something fighter planes, bombers, missiles that go from air to sea, air to air, land to sea, sea to sea, or land. We have mortars, grenades, atomic bombs, nuclear bombs and chemical weapons. Any of these would surely overpower the enemy. Why do we fight with horse and sword?"

Wazeem tried to explain two millennia of the relentless assault on other worlds, now open to attack, as a single moon rose here on Earth.

"In spite of the Valeo victory, we realized the enemy would rise against us yet again, and so we devised a plan to prepare for the next conflict. We collaborated to create this place and worked on it to build fortifications, getting ready for this battle."

"This Fightworld place you mean, Wazeem?" Stacey asked, starting to understand, sort of. "On Earth?"

"Yes, but also no, Mistress Stacey." Wazeem seemed apologetic. "The idea of the design was here on Earth, as it was the last known world, and that the Grimole had laid low for almost two hundred years. 'When' this world is as you see it, but 'what' is probably more appropriate. A different dimension, where the laws of nature are not the same, for we cannot move time backwards or forwards."

"What does that mean, dude?" Sam was confused.

"That everything on Fightworld has to remain on the exact same timeline as when it was first created, no matter what might've happened since, even hundreds of years later," Beth explained.

"And that it's like that for them coming here," Stacey said. "They can't bring their advanced weapons either."

"Exactly," Wazeem said.

"So, no nukes? Got it. But we'll need more manpower," Sam countered.

"Is that right, Wazeem?" Harry asked.

"Master Harry, our defeats outweigh our victories. With every triumph, the enemy prevails while we fall further…" He paused, looking for the right words. "We are now down to but a few worlds remaining while they grow tenfold. There is no stopping their coming. They grow faster than we can drive them back. We now look to Earth for a new way to defeat them. We look to you."

"Jeepers, no pressure!" Sam cried out.

"Stopping their coming is the key," Harry said. "We stop their coming, and we can beat them."

Wazeem looked at him, confused. "But they are already coming, Master Harry."

"We will find a way to stop more of them coming," he replied confidently.

HOURS LATER, AS THEY WENT TO BUNK DOWN AGAIN, HARRY sat beside Wazeem at the fire. "My friend, I want to know if you can help me trial some exercises that could help us in battle."

"Tell me what you want, and I shall see if it's within my ability, Master Harry," Wazeem replied, feeling a little curious.

Harry looked around and saw Sam, Stacey, and Beth were all asleep. He put his right hand over his left in a cup, palms slightly apart, and felt the warmth. Between his hands, a spark started, growing to a small fireball.

"Wazeem," Harry's voice wavered as he tried to hold this uncontrollable expanding atom within his hands, "will you please use any force you have available to contain the power within my hands, but without hurting any of us?"

"Contain, Master Harry?" he asked quizzically.

"Yes, Wazeem, contain, like maybe with a magnetic field, if

you know what that is?"

"Indeed, Master Harry." Wazeem held his hands about three inches on either side of Harry's hands, fingers and palms straight. The area between their hands shimmered with a soft bluish mauve glow, intensifying until a box formed—a perfect cube surrounding Harry's hands: a force field that then lost its blue tone and became pale lilac.

"Excellent, Wazeem!" Harry was ecstatic. "Can you hold it?"

"I think so, Master Harry," he replied, but Harry could see there was pressure on him—too much pressure.

"Okay, enough." Harry wanted to continue, but this was going to take time and practice. "But can we try again soon, please?"

"Certainly, Master," he said.

Wazeem was certainly mystified by these latest events, but intrigued also. More so, his respect of this young human continued to grow.

# Chapter 9

First light they were due to leave, and as they headed back to the Off-G room, they passed a camp with the Japanese Samurai, one of whom Beth recognized as Kyote, a friendly face from their escort to the wall. This was a refreshingly new culture that Harry and Stacey bonded well with.

The Japanese were of a very honorable society, where warriors were highly respected. "Death in honor" was their creed, meaning tribute was even paid to their foes, especially after battle. Their craftsmanship of making swords was second to none, folding metal hundreds of times to make only the strongest, sharpest edge. Their skill at physical fighting was also world class, with martial arts strengthening their arms of sword and dagger.

"Bushido means the way of the warrior, valuing honor,

reckless bravery, and selflessness in duty," their Sensei, Hoshito, said. "It means the Samurai will give up their own life and embrace death."

He passed a handmade three-hundred-year-old sword with crafted leather wrapped handle and forged steel blade to Harry. "Harry san, we offer you our honor with this sword, to live and fight so that our enemy may die by your blade."

The sword had a beautiful black polished scabbard with a sterling silver embossed band. It was certainly a show of Japanese workmanship.

"It is named Fudo Masamune, named after the swordsmith Masamune, who is depicted wielding a sword to cut through ignorance and delusion. It is a katana known for its exceptional craftsmanship and association with the deity of wisdom and fire."

"This is too much. Thank you, Hoshito." Harry stammered out his reply, feeling extremely emotional.

Hoshito bowed his head, accepting the appreciation, and Harry reciprocated to match the gesture in respect.

He then passed Stacey another weapon: a slightly curved dagger of about seven inches long. "This blade, called a tanto, is used for self-defense and close combat or ritualistic purposes. Its name is Juzumaru, which translates to 'Rosary Beads,' named for the gems used to decorate its hilt. It is associated with religious devotion and protection from evil. The bound handle is made from the Sakaki, a spiritual tree of Japan, and it brings sacred belief to physical strength in battle."

It was Stacey's turn to bow with their Sensei in formal tradition.

IT WAS MORE THAN HALF A DAY ON HORSEBACK UNTIL THEY reached the door home. It was also their eighteenth night away, Harry calculated.

They were leaving the garage when a car pulled up, dropping Regina off.

"Mom," Sam greeted her with a hug.

"Sorry, Mom…," Harry started.

Before he could apologize, she chided him, "Nonsense. I've had a great day and I hope you have, too."

The teens were bewildered. "So today you went visiting?" Harry asked.

"Of course, dear. I told you I was. Now, is everyone here for dinner?"

It was still the Wednesday of almost three weeks earlier when they had left. They had been gone almost twenty days but had returned on the same day! Wazeem had been true to his word. Time had certainly slowed. It was hard to comprehend what had happened. Three weeks in nine hours?

Later in the evening, Harry asked Wazeem if he was ready to assist with training again.

With his agreement, they continued with the fire in his hands and the electrical field containing it. As the ball of flame increased, the energy of the box intensified, reddening to become a brilliant lavender.

This time Wazeem was able to hold it longer, and with more control. The contained orb was now able to be held stable for a couple of minutes. As they brought the exercise to a close, Wazeem asked Harry about its purpose and usefulness.

"Well, I'm not sure what the purpose is as yet, but I'm pretty sure once I know how to control it, I'll know how to use it," Harry said.

Wazeem did not seem quite so convinced.

# Chapter 10

On Saturday, they planned to work on their newfound skills, controlling their powers as Wazeem had suggested.

Sam started early on a project in the garage but joined both Beth and Harry to pick Stacey up mid-morning. On their way back, they passed the cinema with signs advertising *Hansel and Gretel*.

"How do they think these things up, I wonder?" Beth asked.

"It was a fairy tale by the Brothers Grimm." Harry couldn't help himself. "Jacob and Wilhelm were German authors. They also wrote *Snow White*, *Little Red Riding Hood*, *Sleeping Beauty*, *Tom Thumb* and *Rumpelstiltskin*." He finished drifting off quietly and a little embarrassed he might've gone too far.

"Of course, the Brothers Grimm," Stacey said more to herself than anyone. "Grimm, Grim, Grimole." She paused, changing the subject. "I wonder what they look like, the Grimole."

"Yeah, well like Yoda of course. You know, big ears, green, wrinkled. Big fangs drooling, not quite so cute, and without the light saber!" Sam quipped from the back seat, laughing.

Stacey picked up on how he had described the *Star Wars* character, putting two and two together. She turned from the front passenger seat and looked at him square in the eyes.

"You know what they look like, don't you, Samuel Porter?"

Sam knew straight away that he had gone too far and tried to dodge her stare but ended up facing Beth instead, who sat beside him. He turned back to the front of the car where he was met by Harry, staring back from the rear-view mirror.

Stacey managed to see Harry's look and exclaimed, "Harry Porter, you and your brother *both* know something you're not telling us!"

"Well, uh…" It wasn't often he was lost for words. Neither, in fact, was Sam, but he was equally befuddled. "Yeah, you see, uh…"

"Yeah, I see, but what do I see?" Stacey was not impressed, and Beth continued to stare down Sam, unblinking.

"Well, there was this dream…," Sam uttered.

"Yeah, I had a dream," Harry mumbled.

"What, you both had dreams?"

"When?"

"What was in them?"

"Was it the same night?"

"The same dream?"

The girls were relentless, and the boys wilted.

"It stood and stared at me, hating me for just being alive. It wasn't of this world, nothing I'd want you to ever meet." Sam shuddered.

Beth reached out and took his hand, and Sam let out a long, slow breath.

"It gave me the creeps, and it was only a dream."

"No, it was more than just a dream." Harry added his account of meeting Ludwig. "It thinks it can beat us, it taunted me," Harry said. "That worried me for a while, but I feel—no, I know—I'm missing something—something about both these dreams. Something important, but I just can't grasp it."

"You'll get it." It was Stacey's turn to take Harry's hand. The four of them rode in silence for a few minutes until she asked, "What happened to the Borgil you were looking at?"

"It's in the old freezer in the garage," Sam answered, again too quickly, without thinking.

"I want to take a look at it," Stacey said in a voice cold enough to match the temperature of the freezer.

"Yeah, I thought you might've said that," Harry said in a neutral tone, but feeling less than excited at the prospect of playing mortician again, especially with the girls there.

Not long after, they were in the garage with the Borgil corpse retrieved from the freezer and on the bench before them for inspection. Still in the black garbage bag from just a week prior, it seemed more like months ago.

Sam opened the bag and dumped the carcass on the wooden work bench. Being frozen meant it didn't smell, but he knew it wouldn't stay that way for long in the humidity of the warm summer's day.

The mongrel's silky black coat remained tinged with blue. The claws and talons, snout, fangs, inky yellow eyes, and elongated ears had not changed. Equally its threat of ferocity and destruction remained, even in death.

"Ugh, it's hideous," Beth gasped.

"Not just hideous, but extremely dangerous." Stacey was acutely aware that this was not just a dog, but a weapon of destruction—a projectile of meaningless worth that the enemy would send in uncountable numbers to wreak havoc on their foe. And that foe was now them.

In a flash, Stacey was in a waking dream. The Borgil overran all defenses at the wall as countless humans and their allies were overpowered, maimed, and killed. She gasped in despair as a swarm of their dogs surged over the walls, with an army of Grimole behind to finish off all that remained. Emitting a cry of anguish, she fell backwards in shock.

Harry, Sam, and Beth all reached out, grabbing her, keeping her upright. The three of them surrounded her with concern until she slowly came about—aware, and yet almost possessed.

"They are but a tool to the Grimole! Nothing more than a bullet, and they have more guns than we can count! We need to find more ways to defend ourselves from these hounds of Hell!"

Nobody noticed Wazeem sitting quietly in the shadows, unseen in the dark, until he rose and spoke in a quiet, even voice.

"My Masters and Mistresses, for the world of men to win this day, it will require the help of your new allies who must work together as one, with whatever means are at your disposal. Humanity will need to unite as never before, and animal, weapon, and magic will all be needed to defeat them, for they are beyond count now. Many shall perish in this battle. We shall lose brothers, sisters, and friends. The four of you shall play a major part, but you must be aware of what it is you are undertaking and recognize that you are an influential force in this epic confrontation. Keep working on your abilities, for it is you who hold the key."

It was quite a speech from the off-worlder. It inspired hope. And hope rallied motivation.

Sunday morning brought sunshine and their meeting with a new ally: the Vallaris.

The third door had their home world "Valeo" scorched into the wood, but as they approached it, Harry called out, "Stop, something is different."

Stacey noticed it first. "There's a sign above the seventh door now!"

Sure enough, there was a new timber sign that had

"Fightworld" etched into it, with a human arm and clenched fist beside it.

"Nice work, Sam!" Beth said.

Indeed, they were all inspired by his handiwork. Sam was pleased, to say the least after his efforts Saturday morning.

The third door opened to a corridor with some sixteen more of various sizes, too large to see the ends.

"The Vallaris have the most soldiers to contribute. They are the largest world to join man," Wazeem explained, opening a double barn-style entrance to a hall four times larger than the one they had entered on Ladon.

Already inside were the Perie royalty of Sari, Aquiel, Issy, and Tyla, waiting with four Lygard and about two thousand soldiers.

The Vallaris was an armored culture, mostly soldiers of the bow, sword, and shield. Their attire and names reminded Harry of studies of ancient Romans. After introductions to their General, a formidable man called Tityus, Harry asked if there was a political contingent for them to meet with.

"No, sir, we live in a martial law," Tityus responded. He was tall, strong, and well-built. His close-cropped beard and hair showed he took pride in grooming, just a small sign he looked after himself, no doubt looked after his men, and was a leader to respect. He was matched by his wife Freya who could have been the reincarnation of Venus, the beautiful Roman goddess of love.

Introductions were made for his other generals and their

wives: Phaethon and Itonia; Butis and Aello; Armes and Usha. These generals and their commodores Janus, Kraken, Thetis, Pistor, and Chaos served as the "Sagitta" or "Arrow." The men dressed in white cloth with scarlet red trimmed capes and gold embellishments.

Three hundred captains and lieutenants wore the same cloth but black and purple.

Like the Sagitta, they had the same gold embellishments and served as the "Medius" or "Center." Both the Sagitta and the Medius had helmets of gold to match their body armor. They wore a sword called a Gladius with a wide blade and had round shields with a large double V cast into it.

The remaining soldiers wore black with bright green and silver. Mostly they had longbows or crossbows and quivers with razor sharp arrows and bolts. They served as the Vallaris "Sagittarius" or "Archers."

Harry and Sam wondered at the highly organized and elegantly dressed array. They meandered around the great hall, meeting varying ranks down to bowmen of both long and cross, as well as cooks, engineers, and all those that worked to keep an army moving forward.

After some small talk of the nature of weapons, they were invited to an exhibition of the bow in a training room off the outer corridor.

A double door that was only slightly less prestigious than the entry revealed a weapons training range. It was an impressive expanse of open ground with hills and trees, complete with mounds and bunkers for targets, all set for the firing of weapons.

"Oh yeah," Beth breathed.

The Vallaris were immensely proud of their skills, showing the entourage marksmanship of both longbow and crossbow. They exhibited an ability to score a perfect bulls-eye time and again from distances of 50 to 150 yards with the bow. The crossbow could match at distances of more than twice that.

The humans applauded them and were requested to try their hand, with their newly acquired off-world abilities.

Sam made a show of using the arrow from the bow hitting the bulls-eye, but it was Issy who, still feeling indignant from Friday said, "Oh, he could hit that at 500 yards with a flame on the fletching."

Beth retaliated in jest to keep the mood light. "Yeah, like Mercury with wings on his feet!" The crowd laughed.

"This is not a competition!" Harry declared.

A quiet settled as Harry and Stacey exhibited a show of magic with arrows hitting the target from distances of 250 yards, bursting into flames as they left the bow. There were gasps of amazement and wonder.

"Do it," Harry instructed Beth. They moved back another 150 yards where she melded her left arm into a long bow as her right arm drew an arrow back and shot a perfect bull once, twice, three times.

"More," Harry insisted.

They moved back to 500 yards where she was handed a crossbow. Taking the weapon, she raised it to her eye, aimed, and then passed it back to the lieutenant. Not needing the weapon she raised her arms, becoming the crossbow and rapidly fired three perfect scores. The Vallaris cheered, and the Perie clapped in approval.

That night, they stayed in rooms off the hall of the Vallaris but Harry and Sam remained awake. The Vallaris were from the world of Valeo but were on a part of Earth that was something of a "virtual Earth." It was almost like a world within a world. The brothers worked on an idea before Sam eventually fell asleep.

Harry, on the other hand, was still wide awake and approached Wazeem for more training.

Cupping his hands, this time Harry tried increasing intensity, instead of size. The fire in his hands was a mere baseball in size, but it burned scorching red-hot. Wazeem's electrical field again brightened, reddening even more to become deep purple. He seemed to have the knack of it, in spite of it being so much more intense.

"Can I try?" Harry asked him. Slowly pulling his hands back, Wazeem watched as Harry assumed control of the outer shield from him. Now increasing the size of the fire, Harry also matched the size of the containment simultaneously, which had become the brightest neon bubble gum color. It positively radiated, encasing what was nothing less than a small meteor inside. Taking a deep breath, Harry's eyes widened.

"The power of the gods within the palms of my hands," he exclaimed in a shaky, wondrous voice.

The exercise over, Harry reduced the fire and shield. Wazeem eyeballed him, for Harry's abilities were growing beyond that of the gift Wazeem had given.

"Master, your abilities exceed even my expectations. You no longer need the power of the Jinni!"

# Chapter 11

Resuming their previous day's session Sam and Harry showed the Vallaris how to double-string a longbow. The accuracy of the Sagittarius improved dramatically, and they were stoked with the result. Their range doubled with no decrease in accuracy.

After shows of their newly improved weapons, the teens gave another display of their skills. Stacey and Harry used telekinesis to "direct" three arrows at a time to the bulls-eyes, again alight with flame.

Sam played tricks with the Vallaris' senses—racing to a target and bringing it up for inspection 500 yards faster than the eye could perceive. Tityus was convinced it was magic, but eventually grasped Harry's explanation.

At the Vallaris' request, Sam undertook hand-to-hand

combat with their strongest soldier, a sergeant called Colossus who looked like a bodybuilder in gladiator's armor. His brute strength was no match for the younger man's speed and agility.

The crowd cheered for their champion but graciously accepted Sam as the victor when his opponent conceded.

Beth handed Sam a bottle of water, giving him a look of approval that he welcomed with a smile and a wink. It was probably a good thing that Issy had sat this day out.

"More!" the crowd called, but Harry had other things in mind. It was time to get to work.

"Generals, will you please join us back in the great hall?" he said.

Shortly after, sitting at a large Vallaris table, Harry revealed the paper plans that he and Sam had been working on the night before.

"Tityus, this is an idea for a simple improvement on the crossbow. We know there are rules as to what can be used in a battle on Fightworld, preventing modern machines, but we believe this one can be constructed, if you are interested." The plans were of a crossbow that could repeatedly fire multiple bolts simultaneously.

"Fightworld?" the general asked, and Sam explained of the name he had given to their new world and the rules about what weapons could be taken there. The general did not know about missiles and tanks but was open-minded to their idea.

"Will it work?" Tityus asked.

"I believe it will," Harry said. "We intend to return tomorrow to make a prototype. If all goes well, we will draw plans for production. Would you like to send a contingent to come with us?"

"It would be Vallaris' honor to accompany you, sire," he replied, bowing.

LATER THAT NIGHT, BETH HAD A DREAM OF HER OWN. SHE gasped at the sight of a Borgil with its front paws over top of her, on her bed, growling and drooling with a ghastly breath that smelled of rotten meat. She considered changing her arms to the Hulk to crush the thing, or a sharp instrument like a giant knife. But what if it still bit her and gave her rabies or something? She decided she was better off to stop time. With the Borgil frozen, she was able to sidle out of bed past the thing. There was another one on the floor behind it! Not wanting to hang around, she moved towards the door, when, out from the shadows jumped another creature—not a Borgil this time but their master.

Green and black, Ludwig the Grimole was everything that Harry had described. He lunged at her, and she collapsed with the Goblin on top, bearing down. His blood-stained lips parted, exposing razor sharp fangs that were only inches from her face, and his beady green eyes devoured her. Beth cringed below him, her chin trembling as Ludwig reveled in her fear.

"It dies!" his hoarse voice scratched out as he leaned forward until they were almost touching noses. Repeating the same words, "It dies," he went to tear her throat out.

She woke with a stifled scream, shaking and sweating. She longed for Sam to be with her and for his arms to be wrapped around her, holding her tight.

EARLY TUESDAY MORNING, THEY MET WAZEEM AND THE Vallaris delegation of generals, commodores, three lieutenants, with twenty Sagittarius through the Fightworld door. They made their way to the camp where the Royal mounted guard waited for their return.

Beth was unusually quiet, but she greeted her mount with enthusiasm. "Hello, Flicka, my beauty," she said as the mare nuzzled her in welcome. "Yes, I've got a carrot for you, my girl."

They breakfasted, and Beth, her spirits lifted by the light of day and the reunion with her beautiful mare, recounted her dream and the encounter with Ludwig. The others listened patiently, and it didn't take long for Sam, who was sitting beside her, to reach over and give her a hug. They held hands tightly as she finished.

Harry felt big-brother outrage at Beth's retelling of her assault, seething inwardly. Stacey held Beth's other hand, squeezing tightly.

"Well, he can say what he likes, but we will prove him wrong!" Stacey said with determination in her eyes.

THE ROYAL GUARD HAD BEEN FOREWARNED THAT THERE WERE more of the enemy coming and had arranged additional rides for the Vallaris and their charge on the journey to the wall.

They were nearly halfway there, walking to rest their steeds and then resumed galloping, when Flicka stumbled, her hoof caught in a rabbit hole. She dropped to the ground with a loud snap and a cry of anguish. Beth threw herself sideways off the saddle and managed to avoid being trapped underneath the horse, but her eyes filled with tears, and she let out a strangled sob as she sank to her knees beside her suffering girl.

"I fear she has broken her leg," Captain Janus said. "There is nothing but compassion for her misery that we can offer."

"You mean kill her!" Beth cried, tears streaming down her face.

"It is better than leaving her to die in agony, Miss," he said, with genuine empathy.

"Wait." Stacey kneeled beside Flicka, soothing her with a low hum while stroking her gently. The hum led to a croon, a song the Perie would know, for the words were not in English.

All watched as she slowly pacified the ailing horse, calming her. But Stacey was losing color, growing drawn and looking weak.

Harry touched her shoulder. "Stace, are you okay? Maybe it's too much?"

Something blue-gray like tentacles extended from her fingers up through her arms to her neck to her face. Looking down he could see the same weirdness happening from her toes up her legs.

"Stace!" he shouted when she didn't respond.

"Keep going, please, Stacey," Beth pleaded. "She's almost there."

Stacey kept stroking the horse for another half a minute and then broke off as the mare jumped up onto all fours and promptly trotted around them in a circle. Then Stacey fainted as the unworldly vein-like fingers dissipated.

Beth stumbled backward with wobbly knees and let out a sigh as Flicka's head shook and neighed. Rising to her feet, Stacey gasped, coming around much to everyone's relief.

The resurrection had the Vallaris look again at the humans in wonder.

Entering the wall, they met to further the prototype of the repeating multi-shot crossbow. Discussions went forward and back; ideas were fronted, rejected, amended, and represented until an agreement was reached.

After a good night's rest by all, engineers, carpenters, bow-makers, and even a piano tuner took part in the project as the teens and their entourage were left to continue relations with the human nations who were either building the wall or waiting within for other members of the alliance to arrive. When finally presented the basic prototype, Sam gasped. It represented a WW2 multi-barrel gun.

"Dudes, that's so cool," he exclaimed.

"Does it work?" Harry asked, trying to hold back his excitement.

"It can fire six bolts simultaneously at a rate of thirty-six per minute, My Lord," the engineer said.

It was the first time Harry had been addressed as such and it didn't sit well. "Friend," he said to the Engineer, "I am merely a commoner and your peer. Please call me Harry."

The bounds of formality set aside, they sat down and discussed the workings of the weapon.

"Flak," Sam said it with authority, naming it after the German origin of a multiple barrel anti-aircraft gun Flakvierling.

The Vallaris around picked up on it. "Flak, Flak, Flak," they chanted, embracing the weapon that they knew would save lives. The bond between man and Vallaris continued to strengthen.

Joining another camp, Sam and Beth met Sheik Amir, an Arabic prince who controlled great reserves of oil and gas. His younger brother Hassan or "handsome" struck a bond instantly with Sam. Hassan was chief of the guard and was charged with the protection of the Sheik. Sam wondered as to why the Sheik would be here, as opposed to just sending his fighters, without risk.

"We are an ancient civilization with old traditions, my

friend," Hassan explained. "Protection of the Sheik not only includes his well-being, but his reputation also."

"So, you are obliged to fight with your men and retain his honor, as well as trying to stay alive?"

"Correct," Hassan said. The Sheik and his brother immediately realized there was more to Sam than met the eye.

"Then we shall have to stay close to you and help keep the Sheik safe. We have ways to help. Some will not be surprising given your knowledge of 21st century weapons, but some will seem like magic."

Both looked at him and Hassan asked, "Magic?"

Sam took a bag of apples and a knife which he cut, quartered, cored, and diced within a fraction of a second.

Taking things further, Beth showed a finger, then two as paring knives. She elongated them to become carving knives like a blender then chopped, sliced, and diced the apples like a late-night TV infomercial.

Sheik Amir's eyes widened as he shook his head, speechless. Hassan leaned in, laughing spontaneously in disbelief before shouting in wonder, "I can't believe it!"

"Please understand, these gifts were given to us by the Jinni," Beth said.

"You have met our Jinni?" Sheik Amir was incredulous.

"Yes, Sheik. He has given us gifts to help defend our nation and yours, this entire world, and others. But we will still need help from everyone here, for the enemy is not like any we have met before."

"And who is this enemy?" Amir asked, narrowing his eyes.

"A darkness like we have never known," Beth said, shuddering at the memory. "An evil parasite that preys not on people or animals, but whole worlds. This time, they think we are theirs for the taking."

"Our death and this world is their prize," Sam answered, feeling the harsh truth deep inside.

They talked for hours with light explanations of the gifts bestowed upon them, growing their relationship. When it was time to leave, Hassan presented Sam with the gift of a Scimitar—a handmade Arabic sword. It was beautifully made with the finest curved steel blade, gem-encrusted handle, including a massive ruby on top, and matching scabbard.

"Akhi," was all Hassan said, which Sheik Amir translated as, "My Brother."

Sam, who was rarely speechless, choked out a stuttered thank you.

# Chapter 12



The morning started with a meeting of Harry, Sam, Vallaris commodores Phaethon and Armes, and the engineers.

Meanwhile Stacey and Beth said they needed to groom the horses. Wazeem elected to join them in one of the battlefront stables.

"I wondered if there was a way we could make the crossbow smaller," Harry said. "You know like a hand-held pistol."

"Yes, my Lord!" Forgetting the earlier agreement, the chief engineer could hardly contain his excitement.

"A single shot reloadable handgun!" another exclaimed.

"That would be epic, dudes," Sam agreed.

"But is such a thing possible?" Armes asked.

"Yes, general—a close quarters weapon that would fire a bolt up to 50 feet accurately."

"Momentous," Sam said. They looked at one another, and then laughed, for this surely was a momentous occasion.

Nearby Stacey and Beth groomed their mares, Flicka and Misty. It was quite cool in the stables with the wonderful smell of oak and straw, and they brushed in slow steady strokes, comfortable in silence, patiently waiting for conversation to come when it felt natural.

Wazeem also brushed his mount in the back stall, remaining silent, sensing there was something he should hear.

"So, I just wondered how you manage to keep everything together, you know, with everything that's going on and all..." Beth started.

Stacey looked at her over Misty's back. "I can't tell you everything will be okay, Beth. These are uncharted times for us, for all mankind, and for those coming to help. But we are gaining strength, finding friends, and gathering momentum."

Stacey paused then continued.

"I also had a dream," she stuttered, not sure she wanted to say anything but needing to share her experience with somebody.

"No, not a dream—a nightmare."

Wazeem listened as Stacey continued. In neighboring Mornington, she had lay in bed, and again like Beth, she had thought she'd been wakened by several Borgil growling and snarling at her bedside. Terrified, she had used her telekinesis to raise them to the ceiling onto one side of the room with the intention of being able to run to the door opposite. Her heart pounded rapidly in her chest as she got out of bed and headed for the door when she was attacked aggressively by a goblin with red eyes glaring like fiery coals in the dark and sharp fangs drooling.

Matching Sam's description, Remus stood about five-and-a-half-feet tall but seemed like a giant in the darkness as he attacked Stacey before she was even aware of what was happening. Gloating over her, the devil pinned her arms and held a sword at her throat, hissing, "It dies, dies, yes it does." Parting his lips, a red-pointed tongue surrounded by blood-stained rows of fangs drooled saliva from above.

Stacey tried to teleport, but she remained pinned in the creature's grasp, smelling his vulgar stench. Heavy on her chest, Remus pushed the edge of the blade against her while he licked his fangs with that disgusting pointed tongue.

"Harry…," she whispered, terrified.

Remus howled, delighted in the moment and repeated, "It dies, it dies," as the blade pushed to her throat.

"All I could think about was Harry and how I'd let him down." Tears formed in Stacey's eyes as she recounted the events of the night before. Was it really only then?

"And I still haven't told him about it because I know it will hurt him, and it will make him angry. But mostly it will distract him. It will take his thoughts away from what he needs to concentrate on—killing those awful things as he is now preparing to do, by joining clans, uniting countries, connecting worlds. My only comfort is that at the end of it, I dreamed Harry joined me;

that he held me and whispered, 'It's okay.' It was only then that I slipped into a dreamless sleep." Stacey paused, trying to regain her composure. "Harry is my 'go-to guy.'"

Tears welled in Beth's eyes.

Stacey continued. "Sam would also be your 'go-to guy,' if you want him to be. Your 'keep everything together guy.' That's your call though."

Beth hugged Stacey. "I really fancy him," she confided.

In the background, Wazeem again wondered at the world of man and admired their support of each other in the face of such adversity.

LATER THAT NIGHT, HARRY AWOKE WITH A START. HE HAD BEEN dreaming about Stacey having the life sucked out of her by tentacles that spread throughout her whole body, right up to her head. Facing away and crouched over her, a figure turned, rising, stretching, and revealing himself. A Grimole of almost six feet rose, black but tinged with yellow, with golden yellow eyes. His appearance was almost ape-like with a flattened face and sloping forehead, his long black hair starting from halfway towards the rear of his head and elongated ruddy ears protruding backwards.

This was a whole new class of fiend. He had a hugely muscular body, and sharply pointed horns grew from his back and claws protruded between his first and second knuckles. He oozed malevolence, vengeance, and cruelty.

With a deathly stare, Rubezahl's voice grated. "She dies, yes she does, dies, she dies." He literally spat the words out, saliva dribbling from his distorted mouth filled with sharp fangs and two massive tusks at the front on the bottom, like that of a wild boar. Transparent membranes unfolded—wings spreading satanically that began to flap like depictions of the Devil himself.

"Share with me, yes share, you share." The demon drooled as an odorless smoke filled the room, which began to fade out as the outside world closed in with visions of…

*What?* Harry wondered. *The future?*

The vision cleared, but the fog remained on the outside, like that of an early black-and-white TV show showing a dream with past events. A playground with families playing on green grass were attacked by grotesque figures half dressed in black loin cloths and leather, wielding sword and dagger. Their skin was gray-green, and elongated heads housed pointed ears and a lipless mouth filled with crooked teeth like that of a vampire. The humanoid abominations laid waste to all, leaving only scorched earth in their wake as they continued throughout the world, repeating their savagery over and over whilst clamoring obscenely.

The fog cleared, and Harry's pulse raced; his skin clammy, his breath ragged and raspy, panting wildly as Rubezahl appeared once again.

"You see, yes see, now you see, you see." The demon was jubilant, noting the look of dread in the human's eyes.

And then the dream faded.

*The Apocalypse. Yes, I see. I see our annihilation!* Harry awoke with a start, recoiling.

Harry couldn't share this dream any more than he could share knowing about Stacey's with Remus and about being there holding her when she finally succumbed to sleep once more. It was all too soon, still too fresh.

He lay awake for hours afterwards, tossing and turning as he tried to come to grips with what he had dreamed.

ANOTHER TWO DAYS OF MEETING MORE COUNTRIES KEPT THEM busy until the next prototype was ready: the hand-held cross-bow. It was a mere ten inches in length and held two bolts—a primary and a spare—both only measuring seven inches. But it had an outstanding power-to-size ratio. Unlike a normal cross-bow, the cables ran vertically rather than horizontally, meaning it didn't have much width and could be housed in a holster on the leg or side under the shoulder.

With a flick of a small switch, it would swap between the primary and spare bolt, and the initial tests showed 100 percent accuracy to seventy-five feet. Harry and Sam couldn't have been more rapt, and everyone applauded the new weapon, aptly named the hand-bow.

The commodores, captains, and lieutenants of the Vallaris loved it, so orders were issued for its immediate production—one for every soldier not carrying a long or crossbow.

Before leaving Fightworld, the teens were introduced to their "Royal Guard" who were assigned to protect them in this darkest hour.

"But we are neither royal nor even of political importance," Harry protested, a sentiment which was reiterated by Sam, Beth, and Stacey.

"Maybe not, my Lord," an English Royal Guardsman answered, "but we have orders from the leaders of many countries, and ahem," he coughed, "other worlds," he finished, a little shakily.

"There will be one-hundred-and-fifty warriors surrounding you, made up of twenty-five of the most elite forces from nations of Earth: Japanese Ninja, English Hussar, Hashasian, Ghurkha brigade, The Norse Varangian Guard, and The Immortals, thought long deceased, but deemed immortal as their fallen were replaced after every battle."

Knowing there was no winning this, they met their sentinel in person, respecting them all one by one. It was awkward for them, as they felt their position was overstated, but word had quickly spread that they wielded magical powers and that they had the mental prowess to develop new weapons or skills and the political aptitude to unite worlds. Without realizing it, they had become Earth's elite, their own Guardians, with royalty an inessential title.

Leading their mounts up the inner wall, they saw a mass of black figures in the distance—thousands, no tens of thousands.

The figures surrounded rudimentary structures that were hard to make out, but appeared to be wooden mobile stairwells, ladders, and catapults even, to throw stone or fire.

"So many!" Stacey gasped.

"Already they prepare for war." Harry looked to Wazeem. But the Jinni did not reply. His lack of response cemented what Harry already knew: time was now against them.

On the way back to the door, Stacey asked General Phaethon about their last encounter with the Grimole; the numbers that fought and those that had died.

As Stacey was a woman, the general would normally have been taken aback. But this female was truly a warrior equal to those of the Perie Royals and therefore she earned his respect.

The general recounted the last war on his home world of Valeo, where over a hundred thousand Vallaris fought alongside other worlds including Ladonians, Perie, Xanthu, and Uranians.

"Why was there no one from Earth to fight alongside you?" she asked.

Wazeem joined the conversation. "Because the known Universe did not include Earth then, Mistress Stacey."

"There were about ten thousand Ladonians, four thousand Perie with forty thousand Lygard, two thousand Xanthu, and six Uranians. We fought on our farms, in our villages, and our families fought and died with us." The General's voice was that of a sorrow that could never heal. "There were maybe a hundred and fifty thousand Borgil and fifty thousand Grimole."

"But there will be more this time. A lot more," Wazeem said grimly.

Stacey felt sick to her stomach.

The general continued. "We drove them back, but they kept coming, relentlessly. Even with the home advantage, we struggled in the face of their sheer hatred for us. Why do they despise us so much? What have we done to them?" Phaethon's voice seemed to question defeat.

But Stacey's reply was assertive, filled with human spirit and deep emotion. "Because they are ungodly. They are not of this world, and their objective is universal, not global annihilation. We need to be as prepared for anything and everything as we can be—to make sure this next battle, this final battle, ends it once and for all."

The more she talked, the more it inspired the general.

"How many more Vallaris do you expect will join us?" she asked.

"Another seventy thousand will defend our ranks, Miss," he replied.

*The odds are still well stacked in their favor,* she thought, thanking the General and mulling it over, riding alone in silence. This battle was going to be fought on the world of man, and it was going to need every last one of them. It was a somber realization.

# Chapter 13

They returned home, and although it was five days later, it was still Tuesday. They retired early, unsure what the morning's arrival would bring. Upon waking, Wazeem informed them that Sari had requested they return to the Perie hall. A little mystified, they entered the great hall where the Perie Royals waited.

"My friends," the queen greeted them, "we have heard of your latest travels and exploits."

*Uh-oh,* Stacey thought.

"You have helped develop new weapons to aid us all, as well as making bonds with nations and outer worlds to increase the numbers of the Alliance. We are very proud. We of the Perie have decided we would like to gift each of you a Lygard—your own personal champion to love and to lead."

"My Queen," Stacey stammered, "we cannot accept such an offering. The Lygard are the foundation of the Perie, and yours alone. We could not possibly…"

Her voice tapered off as Tyla interrupted. "Stacey, this is a great honor. No Lygard has ever been given by the Perie in all our history, and it was not a decision made lightly. Sari, Aquiel, Issy, and I have all agreed on this."

"Your highness, we gratefully accept." Beth did her best to keep her voice even despite her excitement.

"Yes, your Majesty," Sam and Harry agreed in unison.

Aquiel brought forward four of their faithful guard.

"Beth, this is Rogue. She, as her name suggests, is a bit of a rascal, so you will have to watch her, but she is loyal and will love you unconditionally." Beth immediately hugged Rogue as well as the Royals.

"Stacey, this is Belle," Tyla continued. "Belle means beauty, but of course you can see that. She, too, will love you absolutely, and we know you will love her in return."

Stacey could not believe how the Perie had managed to make choices that were so befitting. She also gave them a hug, full of tears and gratitude.

"This is Zeus, Harry. You will know his name is of Greek mythology and translates to 'sky' but is the mainstay God of the sky and thunder. He rules the Gods. Zeus will give his life to protect you."

Harry was overwhelmed by the honor of their gift. The

Lygard reflect the inner strength of the Perie, and Zeus was clearly a purebred of royal lineage. Harry was humbled and thanked them sincerely.

"Sam, this is Deuce. His name means two, because he is a brother to Zeus. He also has power and strength, and he will defend you like all Lygard do. We know you will love him."

Sam was speechless, a very rare occurrence for him.

Later, while spending time with their charges in a secluded corner of the hall, they contemplated the responsibility of looking after the Lygard, discussing their needs: beds, food, grooming. There was also the matter of keeping their "off-worldness" from friends and family.

"We go to Urania in the morning," Harry said, rubbing the thick coat of Zeus' neck. "I don't think we should take them with us."

Wazeem agreed. "This has been truly remarkable, Master Harry. The Lygard are protected with pride and passion. They have never been gifted. It shows support and solidarity from the Perie, but maybe it is better they wait for your return. It will only seem like moments to them."

They acknowledged his opinion and enjoyed their time with the new Lucanine additions, but Harry was conflicted, trying to decide if this was the right time to talk about dreams again, or to not ruin the moment. He decided he couldn't wait, and the mood faded when conversation resumed.

There was a grim look on Harry's face. His manner was

dour, and the others could tell he had something serious to say.

"Dreams," he started, almost choking the word out, "are more than just images in our subconscious, like we used to think. We have had episodes of telepathy—times where we have contacted each other by thought alone." He paused, took a breath, and then continued. "Four times our dreams have been real experiences of actually being visited by the Grimole."

They could all see he had more to say but was having trouble saying the words.

Stacey could tell he was anxious and clicked onto something he had said. "Four times? I know there was your original one with the Borgils and Ludwig, Remus with Sam, Beth with Ludwig, but what was the fourth?"

Harry gave her a grim, knowing smile. "I know about Remus, Stace. I know that he came to you. I know what he said, how he looked, even how he smelled and how he made you feel. And what that did to you. I know your fear, and I hate that, but mostly I hate your unwillingness to share this because of how it might affect me."

"You either know what I'm thinking, or Beth told you what I said, and I know she wouldn't do that." Stacey was adamant.

"I seem to know more than I should," he replied honestly, feeling the pressure of emotion falling on him. "And Beth didn't say anything, Stace. I just know."

"Then you were really there, holding me and whispering, 'it's okay' as I fell asleep." It wasn't a question.

"Yes," he said, holding her eyes, "because you called me."

Stacey didn't just catch Harry's stare. She locked his gaze, and they were almost hypnotized.

Biting her lip, her cheeks glowed as her hands fidgeted, but the tears fell, betraying her in the end.

Harry took her hands into his and responded in kind with a gentle squeeze, his chin trembling as he looked for the words to apologize. No words were needed as Stacey preempted his emotion, but Harry's admission of guilt was still pending.

"What is it?" Stacey asked.

He looked on the verge of tears, accepting the blame because he hadn't been able to protect her from her ordeal.

Stacey responded immediately with a hug, wrapping both arms around her guy. "No more secrets?"

He smiled at her but knew there was still another dream he hadn't managed to share as yet.

# Chapter 14



WEDNESDAY BROUGHT AN EARLY MORNING SHOWER THAT cleared with more muggy summer heat. Entering the last door named "Urania" Harry noticed the word "*Immemorialis*" below—small words hardly visible until you were right below the sign. The corridor inside only had two doors, and as they entered the first, he said, "'In-memorialis'. It means…"

Copping a look from Sam, he smirked and summed it up with, "very old."

"Immemorial indeed, young mortal." A man three inches shy of six feet stood before him wearing a dark gray cloak with a hood covering white hair that matched his long white beard. He was old—no, he was ancient—and although not overly tall, he was imposing all the same.

"Harry, these are The Ancients, and this is Mordred, the

Ere," Wazeem introduced them.

"The first, yes, I understand," Harry replied. "Mordred, thank you for coming; it is good to meet you."

An introduction of the rest of the teens was somewhat of a formality, as the Elders seemed to know who they were already.

Somehow, Harry also knew who these Uranians were, although he didn't know how that could be.

"Morphius, Plaga, Necromancer, Pluvius, it is good to meet you also." He greeted them in cloaks that stretched from head to toe in gray or black, all deeply hooded.

"I see your species has evolved since we last met," Mordred said, looking at Harry. "Welcome, Adam's sons and daughters. We are the Immemorial of Urania."

"Yes, you walked among our forefathers a millennium ago," Harry replied. "Walked among men, and yet not with them."

Mordred eyed him with interest, but Harry wasn't finished.

"You have a lifetime of knowledge men do not, and your magic can do what we cannot. We would surely appreciate your help now."

Mordred gave a look of approval for the young human, something uncommon for Uranians, surprising even Wazeem.

But to Mordred, this new species inspired him, offering more than they would take, and ready to sacrifice themselves for others unconditionally. They knew these humans, and there was no need for a show of their talent. Or at least Mordred thought so…

Morphius had a dark beard tinged with ginger but no gray.

His cloak had a long hood and his face was covered with veins that throbbed dark brown like the roots of trees. There was lightning that could have been tattoos or something mystical, and light beads of gold glowing within the skin on his face, neck, and forehead. He held back—not shy, just reserved.

Beth was anything but! She greeted him in her natural way, even taking his grizzled hand when it changed to a claw and matching it with her own ability to transform, bonding in a way he had never known, not even with those of his own race. His eyes changed from bright blue to gray, and Beth matched him; then to hazel brown to black, and she matched him again before they both settled on a brilliantly clear, luminous green.

It made Morphius seem even more intimidating and yet simultaneously more amicable to her. He pulled back and brought forward a creature with four legs, then six, then eight. It had a tail, one head and then two, firstly that of a dog, and then that of a lion. It shimmered as it changed from one form to another.

"The Metamorphan—a changeling from a time ago," Morphius proclaimed. "I shall teach you to bring about such a weapon against the Grimole and their cur."

There was clearly a bond between the two, and Beth's emotions took hold as she thrust out her chest, and tears welled, very proud of herself.

A warmth radiated through Morphius' body, and he reached out, taking her hand in his own, as he accepted his new Earthly ally.

Then came Pluvius—the next sorcerer deemed as "normal" by Uranian standards with the classic hooded cloak, white hair, and beard.

"Pluvius—of rain." Harry quoted more Latin, keeping the trend alive. As he offered his hand in greeting, lightning blazed between them, surprising them both.

Pluvius demonstrated his namesake with a torrential downpour, following with bolts flashing and thunder roaring.

Harry drew power from his hands and threw flame into the blaze that exploded into small fireballs. The fireworks display was spectacular!

Enthralled, they drummed their feet on the hard ground as they clapped and cheered, hooting and yelling in a synchronized, almost melodic "we will rock you" fashion.

Pluvius pledged his support to the earthlings, but with one condition. "I will support you if Plaga supports you," he said.

Necromancer was the most forbidding of the Uranians at more than seven feet. Although he was one of the Ancients, Harry realized that he was different, in many ways. He was dark, conjuring, and Harry could feel the occult.

The blood coursed through Harry's veins in a mixture of excitement and trepidation as he said, "The Necromancer definition is someone who practices black magic—a wizard."

"We have no business with your world," the Uranian replied bluntly.

Harry approached him, wary that this could undo all the

good work that they had already achieved.

"You are Druids," he said with respect. "You arrange magic, sorcery, and theurgy. These are tools that would help us, for there is no one left but us to fight and defend not only our world, but all of the other last remaining worlds—even Urania."

After a brief pause considering his words, Necromancer replied, "Your point is valid, but it is too late. The enemy comes as we speak, and this time they are more than numerous: they are uncountable. The odds are too great, for man cannot win this battle."

"Maybe," Harry rasped. "But we have many friends to help, and we have to try. If we don't fight, we all die!" He was getting angry—worse, infuriated—something that was quite new for him. For years he had taken the bullying of Brad Ogilvie and company at school with mild annoyance, but Stacey's encounter with Remus had opened doors to emotions he had never known: rage, frustration, and hatred.

Just as he was about to give up, Stacey reached out to Necromancer. "Please help us. Every world is relying on us to help them, and you could make the difference."

"Please?" Beth added in support.

The Konjurer spoke again. "If all Uranians agree, then I will help you. And the Necro will favor you. But only if my brothers support you."

They took this as a win, with maybe three out of five on their side now.

As they thanked him, Harry realized he had to be wary of his explosive emotions that threatened to rise. To be too angry or too emotive could mean a loss of control, and that could cost support—support they dearly needed.

Plaga stood back, less interested in this association than even Morphius had been. He was lightly bearded but heavily cloaked like a monk of old, with a hood covering his head and most of his face barely visible. He radiated death, despondence, and despair.

Not perturbed by his looks, Stacey approached him, and without touching him physically, reached out mentally. She tried to assume the pain of Plaga, not even sure it was working, but then felt wave after wave of torment, suffering, and anguish. Getting close enough to see behind the hood she saw his face swelled and pulsated, bulging and then returning to normal, first in one area and then another: left temple, right cheek, left chin, right forehead, right chin over and over. His eyes were dark and sorrowful as she took his hand.

The connection was instant and certainly no less than that of Beth and Morphius, as Plaga connected with her.

*"Plaga is old-world Latin for stroke or wound,"* she quoted Harry. *"Derived from the Greek word Plaga, also meaning strike. How does this relate to you?"*

*"I have the ability to strike a wound without touching,"* the Uranian answered.

*"Strike?"* she asked.

"*Create pain from disease. I am death, and all who face me are dead*," he replied with a sadness of twenty lifetimes of misery.

"*We will help with that*," Stacey replied, but not yet sure as to how.

There were no words spoken, for the whole conversation was telepathic communication and between them alone. To the others, they were just looking at each other, but it was obvious a relationship had formed.

Plaga took her hand and merely said, "Piskies."

"Piskies, um, pardon?" Stacey asked.

"Help them," he replied cryptically.

"But we are the ones who need help; that's why we are here: to seek *your* aid." She wasn't confident in his response, and she looked sideways at Harry, quizzically.

"You help them, and we will help you," was all he would say until Stacey agreed, and then things started to spin in a smoky haze. When Harry grasped her hand, she knew that this reality was going down the rabbit hole, into the unreal.

THE WORLD THEY KNEW FADED AND REAPPEARED AS A MOSTLY barren land of mud huts like igloos, but in a desert surrounded by termite-like mounds two to five feet high that were open to the sky above.

*Almost like chimneys or maybe escape hatches for something unthinkable below*, Stacey thought.

The hot sun burned bright in the sky with two moons reflecting, confusing the visitors who met an indigenous being called Kama in the sandy paths of the town Jemmayl.

At just over two and a half feet tall, with wide eyes and elongated ears, he was alternately brown or white.

"Like a Gremlin, LOL!" Sam exclaimed, having just arrived unannounced and startling them both.

"Uh, yeah, hello guys," Beth added, stepping in beside Sam.

"Maybe feed them after midnight?" Sam offered.

Beth caught his surprised, wide-eyed look and giggled.

Kama looked up in interest but spoke perfect English, introducing his brother Khlama before inviting their new guests into his home.

"We are not your Cremlins!" he proclaimed, kicking Sam in the shin. "We are Piskies!"

"Piskie by name and pesky by nature," Sam said, rubbing his shin theatrically while smiling and winking at Beth, who laughed good-naturedly. He was still mesmerized by her brilliant green eyes.

"We know of your troubles," Kama ignored them, "and we would gladly support you, but for the woes of our own."

"Maybe we could help each other, Kama?" Stacey's raised eyebrows and pursed lips suggested concern. She had always shown a motherly instinct, not lost on the others and now obvious to these new acquaintances.

"Help how?" Kama replied. "We are besieged by creatures

of the night who rise from the bowels of the earth to strike from the darkness above. Predators in the hundreds and thousands that carry off the young and the old, the weak and lately even the strongest of us into the unknown of blackness and an unthinkable end."

He paused with his eyes wide and tears forming as he tried to convey such unimaginable horror. Beth grasped Sam's hand with hers, clammy from cold sweat, as Harry hugged a trembling Stacey beside him, her throat dry and breath uneven.

"Maybe with science," Harry suggested. "But it will take time."

They bedded down for the night as Harry formulated a plan, before sharing his idea.

At first light, they moved out to the mounds with packs of supplies, compact shovels, and jerrycans of water.

At each earthy chimney, they proceeded to use surrounding dirt with the water they carried to make mud-cakes, awaiting Harry's instruction, who cupped his hands with the familiar glow, once again becoming an atomic force of matter. He sent his "gift" down the shaft of the first mound followed by the muddy seal which capped it and was followed by a small explosion that rocked them gently.

The air was filled with the blood-curdled howls from the depths below, screaming in death and defiance. Harry moved to the next mound, delivering his explosive package, and then the next, and the next.

The days were unusually short here and by nightfall, the

usual predatory howls of those underground had become cries of anguish. But these were only the closest of the mounds, and there were many, many more.

Morning brought a rising sun that seemed to shine brighter, burn fiercer, and with it came exuberant energy and jubilation from the Piskies, with Kama, Khlama and some sixty others whooping loudly, all jumping up and down talking in almost gibberish babble as they joined the outworlders.

"Defiance at last!" a three-foot black, brown, and white Piskie with orange streaks named Ginger yelled, peering over the shoulder of Khlama.

"Rebellion!" another echoed, and then a chorus began supporting their cause.

"Survival!" another yelled.

Their words were not lost on him, but with what seemed like a riot beginning, Harry called for quiet. When calm prevailed, he explained that although there had been success, the number of mounds outnumbered a realistic ability to destroy their enemy.

"And this enemy?" he asked. "Do you have a name for them?"

"Nightslayers!" the Piskies cried in fear, in unison.

"They appear from the stacks as the light begins to fade." Khlama's lips trembled, cringing like he was ready to bolt if he saw a shadow move. "We think they have ways to see in the dark, but not eyes like us."

"Like a bat, maybe?" Beth suggested.

"I do not know what a bat is, miss." Khlama's already enlarged eyes bulged, and tears welled as he continued. "In the beginning, they only came in the dead of night, mostly taking our pets, but occasionally a Piskie or two would just disappear."

Looking fondly at his pet Draggo, he introduced Sherpa, who looked like something between a miniature sheepdog and Retriever cross at just over two feet high, with giant floppy ears, an elongated snout, but with a snake-like tail, pointed like a dragon's.

*Dragon meets dog?* Stacey wondered.

"Our cats all vanished," he continued, "and then it became at dusk as the sun set. And when we learned to escape them, they changed it up—coming into our homes when the shadows grew longer with their razor-sharp teeth biting, claws stabbing, and hooked tails goring…and the most terrifying of sounds: tak-a-tak, tak-a-tak, tak, tak, tak, tak-a-tak, tak-a-tak…"

They all shuddered, more than a little unnerved by the noises Khlama repeated way too accurately.

"We think it's a clicking of their gullet in a frenzy, and that we are the meat they take for their hatchlings to feed on," he sobbed, shaking uncontrollably.

Stunned, Harry replied strongly, "Then we need a new plan to combat the Nightslayers." But a slight quiver in his voice betrayed his optimism.

"I have an idea," Stacey suggested.

All eyes turned to her as she stood tall and called to Beth to join her.

She reached out, taking Beth's hands. Sparks started between them, igniting and becoming fingers of yellow and orange burning, scorching red hot until they separated with flames leaping from their hands, controlling fire together and yet independently.

Beth looked up at Stacey, breathing rapidly, with her eyes wide and mouth open in an *aha* moment, for only now was she truly aware that she did not know the full extent of her abilities—not hers, nor Stacey's, or even maybe the boys'. She clutched her fists as her body squeezed tightly, her eyes sparkling and her face beaming.

"So, a new plan," Stacey said, her deep brown eyes burning like a molten rock lake inside a volcano. "We burn the Nightslayers!"

"Burn, yes burn them, burn them all," Beth echoed, mesmerized by Stacey as the flames intensified and the sparks flew like fireworks between them.

The Piskies shouted, "Freedom, Freedom, Freedom," in unison, in favor of any support they could muster to free them from the nightmarish predator that plagued them.

Harry's brow wrinkled, fretting as he looked at Sam.

Sam's strained neck muscles reflected Harry's concern at this new dark side of the girls. They knew Stacey and Beth were both of strong will, and freeing the Piskies from their oppressors had become a new cause, despite the troubles back home. Or perhaps because of it.

AT FIRST LIGHT, THEY MOVED TO THE OUTER MOUNDS WHERE Stacey and Beth bonded, creating fire that they sent to the depths of the underworld and spreading like wildfire in a dry cornfield. The howling made their blood run cold and their skin crawl, albeit also somewhat exhilarating as they exacted retribution on this perverted version of flying dinosaurs during the shortened daylight hours.

The fire spread and the flames intensified as smoke appeared from more and more mounds in the distance, with the occasional creature flying into the sky, slowly flapping their giant wings as they screamed, ascending into the darkening horizon. With grotesquely transparent wings and veins like tentacles, razor sharp rows of teeth and honed talons two feet long, they had eyes of black coal that reflected death.

But from behind them, the light of day gave way to the night, and one of the Nightslayers descended, swooping from the horizon as it burned with fire. Mad with rage and pain, it slammed into Sam's back: seven hundred pounds at thirty miles an hour with the force of a tank, driving him to the ground whilst grasping him in its claws and dragging him head-first through the sand before continuing a path upward into the darkening sky, black from thick smoke.

Harry looked in disbelief and shouted out to Wazeem. "Can't you pull him back?"

Stacey shook violently as anxiety threatened to take over, terrified.

Knowing the moment was hers, Beth rallied, tossing her head in defiance like a mustang in the corral, staring down the cowboys trying to tame it. She pushed her shoulders back and jutted her chest forward, raising her arms and sending first one, then a second, and then a third fireball at the Nightslayer until it fell from the sky. The alien raptor fell like a stone, but still clung to its prey in one last act of defiance.

They rushed to where they thought the landing zone could've been and were relieved to see Sam rise, brushing off dust from the fall, suggesting it was just another day at the office.

"Well, it was a bumpy ride," he joked.

"Samuel Porter!" Beth stared at him. "You nearly died!"

Sam looked at her and put any further jokes aside when he saw her concern. He responded with silence, accompanied by a look of gratitude that won the day. And her heart.

LATER, IN THE TOWN HALL, THEY JOINED MORE THAN A THOUsand Piskies celebrating.

"Umm hey, did you add water to them?" Beth whispered to Sam.

Sam burst into laughter, trying to compose himself as everyone turned and stared. He gave Beth a sideways glance that said "nice one" and received an image from her of a laughing emoji. It made him smile despite himself. But then he wondered what was going on with their connection that was what, now telepathic?

Dawn brought the fiery sun, and they braced to leave the Piskies, with Stacey hugging Kama and Khlama, all with tears streaming. She was an emotional girl, and her struggle was very transparent, but they had troubles of their own to deal with.

"We will return, little ones," Wazeem addressed the Piskies, "but we must go now."

Sam noticed a quiver in his voice. "Dude, are you tearing up too?" he asked and then cleared his throat, feeling a little emotional himself.

Wazeem's dark face seemed to redden, almost to blush a little, and his chin dipped. Beth gave Sam a "back- off" look, kind of smiling.

Stacey bonded easily with the Piskies, assuming them as her charge, but she had also developed feelings for their Jinni, who she had grown to respect.

"It is time to go," Harry said, offering a smile and grabbing her hand. Then things started to spin as they spiraled away.

# Chapter 15

BACK IN THE OFF-G ROOM ONCE AGAIN, THEY GREETED THEIR Lygard with enthusiasm.

Then Sam raised a question they had all been wondering about. "What are the Necro, Dr. Encyclopedia?"

Harry was on it. "Necro comes from the ancient Greek word Nekros, or corpse. It means dead. What he was talking about is anybody's guess."

"Yeah, well, he sure isn't going to be the life of the party." Sam was forever trying to lighten the mood, but there was disquiet in Harry again.

"You're holding back on us, aren't you, Harry?" Stacey asked, already knowing the answer. "Should we talk about dreams, maybe?"

There was no prolonging this any further. Stacey was so

onto him.

"Tuesday night," he stuttered, getting some solace from patting Zeus, who seemed to offer equal comfort in return.

"There were no Borgil, just a Grimole but not like Remus or Ludwig. It was big and menacing. I mean Ludwig was ugly and Remus was intimidating, but this was evil, demonic. A step above."

"Or below," Stacey said. "Rubezahl."

Harry didn't want to look at her, but she took his chin in her hand and forced his stare.

"What did he say?" she asked.

Harry couldn't repeat the words, but he also couldn't lie to her. "Death," he answered simply.

Stacey knew there was more but didn't push it. There would be another time to ask him, another day when it wouldn't upset him so much.

Something still eluded Harry—something about these dreams he knew mattered—but he still couldn't pinpoint it, and that bothered him even more.

The bars of a song came to mind: lyrics like something about selling dreams.

*Yeah, I've got dreams I'd like to sell,* Harry thought glumly.

SUNDAY MORNING WAS ALL ABOUT PREPARATION TO LEAVE FOR Fightworld. The mood was serious and determined. These goodbyes to friends and family could be their last, but there was no turning back now.

*We are leaving for war,* Stacey thought grimly.

Sam, Harry and Beth all looked at her, either reading her face or her mind, but either way one hundred percent in agreement.

Packed and ready to go with Zeus, Belle, Deuce, and Rogue at their side, they entered the seventh door for what they knew could be the last time.

What lay in front of them came as a complete shock. It was the same landscape, but hordes of people moved towards the wall with their horses, carts, and belongings. The road train stretched as far as the eye could see, over hill and round knoll, hundreds and thousands and more.

"Mankind is responding!" Sam shouted, pumped.

Humanity had definitely answered, with countries from every corner of the planet traversing to the wall that would be their defense—to protect their world, and that of the others who were coming to help. The cavalcade excited them, galvanizing them into action.

Greeting their horses once again, they saddled up.

Riding west, Stacey pulled astride of Harry, content not to talk for a mile or two. But eventually she spoke, her words chosen very carefully. "Why couldn't you tell me you were there after Remus came into my dream?"

Harry stared into her deep brown eyes that mirrored his blue ones—windows to their souls, he used to say—and he answered honestly. "Because I couldn't admit that I was there, but not when you needed me." His eyes filled with sadness. "I was too late."

Stacey reassured him that it wasn't his fault—that he did come and the devilish fiend was gone, but she knew there was more. "Why do they visit us in our dreams?" she asked. "You alluded to something you couldn't quite put your finger on. What was that?"

Harry thought about it, and then said he simply didn't know yet.

But Stacey pushed harder. "Why didn't you tell me about your dream with Rubezahl?"

This time, Harry was quick to respond. "It was just too soon. I needed to process it."

"Process it?" she asked.

Harry just nodded, looking ahead.

Riding together, with Rogue and Deuce beside, Beth pulled alongside Sam. They also rode in silence for a while, with some sideways glances and the odd smile. Sam was unusually shy. Eventually Beth broke the quiet, asking him if he was going to ask her to be his girl.

"Well…" he stammered "I, uh…"

"You what, Sam Porter? You were waiting for the right time? The right girl? You've only tried to date me a dozen times. Is a girl supposed to wait forever?" On that last line, Beth gave a smile that would win over Court Judge, Defense Attorney, and

Police Prosecutor combined.

"Kiss me," she said, not asking at all.

Sam moved Joker with a slight tap of his heels, pulling alongside Flicka. He leaned over and kissed Beth. Their first kiss was the kiss of all kisses. The love story that was the reason books had words, songs composed harmony, and poems rhymed.

Beth's chest heaved as her heart pounded, pulling back gasping, laughing euphorically and holding Sam's steady gaze.

"Wow," was all she needed to say, smiling.

"Wow yourself." Sam let the moment stay cool, his own ribs squeezing tight with a rapid heartbeat as his body temperature skyrocketed and heart raced.

A little while later she pulled astride Stacey, relaying the moment with her eyes sparkling and giggling like a grade three schoolgirl. Stacey was thrilled for her.

Laughing and whooping loudly, she squeezed Stacey's hand before kicking her heels, and sent Flicka into a wild gallop, chasing down Sam.

ARRIVING AT THE WALL, THEY WERE YET AGAIN AMAZED, THIS time at the progress that had been undertaken since their last visit. Work had transformed what had already been impressive, with secondary battlements on either side of all three gates. The north gate also had towers on either side and additional barracks with stables included behind. They also saw many camps of human cultures joined by the Vallaris, Ladonians, Perie, and Xanthu.

Tityus, Phaethon, Butis, and Armes welcomed them enthusiastically.

"Look at the new battlements!" Phaethon shouted. "They are for the Flak! They work, and we have many!" The Vallaris had camped with men on the northwest sector, and there were bowmen on all of the Flak battlements, manning the multi-shot crossbows.

They also met the Scots, with Kurkri, and the Ladonians who just happened to be camped beside them. "Laddie, we seem to have many things in common." Lachlan, the Scottish Highlander, clapped him on the shoulder with a massive hit. Sam took the blow in good spirits.

"Aye, my boy," Minor said, with Tross joining them. "Ale!" he shouted out, and they laughed.

Xanthu were stationed on the east joined by men, while Ladonians were on the northwest, again supported by men in reserve behind, protecting the steep cliffs of the ocean to the south. The number of men was a massive surprise. No longer thousands, there were tens of thousands in every camp, and still they continued to come!

They spent the night camped close to the north gate where the main attack was expected, with the steeper terrain of the east and west.

Early morning brought the Perie.

"Men have come!" Sari greeted them with Aquiel and an escort.

"Yeah, they have answered our call to arms," Stacey agreed. "With the Lygard, we number about three hundred and fifty thousand now," Stacey calculated.

"And they are still coming," Harry added, looking at Sari directly.

A further account was taken of the wall, battlements, soldiers, and company. Sectors fortified by six worlds now joined as one: Ladon, Xanthus, Valeo, Urania, Perie, and Earth.

*Six worlds remain—no seven, for Grimorium is also a world,* Harry thought.

"A world no different to ours, just a world that has different principals of physics, but still physics all the same," he said, to no one in particular.

Stacey, Sam, Beth, and Wazeem all stared at him, unsure what to say. Their Royal Guard were someway off, and the Perie Royals were outside of earshot.

"Umm, bro, what was that all about?" Sam asked.

"If we can understand the physics of their world and how it connects to ours, we might be able to find a way to break that portal, or even better—we take advantage of it and disrupt them on their own world."

"You may be right, Master Harry. Their dimension still has laws of physics, albeit different laws from Earth," Wazeem said.

Harry was aware that he had touched on something

important, and yet it still remained elusive.

THE WORKS ON THE WALL HAD ESCALATED RAPIDLY IN THEIR absence. There was now a finished west gate with a deep trench meandering around the entire embankment, including draw-bridges over all three gates. The central north gate was larger than the other two and oversaw them in an elevated position. It was superior, with additional defenses, barricades, and facilities. In fact, the whole defensive formation had come together im-pressively, and spirits were high as they inspected it with a dele-gation of other nations. There were even flags of Sam's clenched fist and pumped biceps—a new united mankind symbol.

As they were returning up the hill to the main gate, Harry noticed something in the distance.

"To the north!" he shouted.

Dark gray thunderheads were rolling in over what looked like an ant's nest in the distance—a blackness that was alive, moving and growing. Stacey saw Harry's concern, and a feeling of dread overcame her. The others followed his look and realized what they were looking at was the imminent invasion.

They raced to the gate, gaining security within the wall and meeting the Vallaris military leaders from the west, the Perie Royals from the east, and Uranian Druids who were now sta-tioned at various sites: Pluvius on the east, Plaga the west, and Morphius north, with Necromancer and Mordred in reserve to support, whilst also watching the Southern Sea.

The enemy was moving quickly as they spread out, and the horizon darkened inky black. Their numbers were growing phenomenally. No longer tens of thousands, there were hundreds of thousands of them. And with them came a foul odor.

*The smell of death,* Stacey thought.

Harry felt the crawling icy grip on the nape of his neck as a feeling that their enemy was trying to lure him into the darkness, but braving his fear, he cried out at the top of his lungs, "Prepare for war!" There was no shaking, no quiver to his voice. He was assertive, commanding.

"To arms, to arms!" Sam echoed in support.

The Royal Guard quickly surrounded them—the best of the best, the elite. They assumed positions to defend their charge and maintain honor. Ninja, Hussar, Arabic Hashasian, Nepalese Gurkha, and Varangian all took arms, prepared to defend them, at any cost.

"Battle stations!" Sari screamed, and the Perie responded. They readied their Lygard with divisions to lead on two fronts: the east and north main gate. They had been down this road before and knew the cost of what was to come. Proud of their role, they didn't just lead the Lygard, they loved them and respected them as they assumed the spearhead of the assault. Many cried, whispering words of encouragement into their ears and patting or hugging them lovingly.

The Xanthu prepared their jungle friends in much the same

way, while the Ladonians and Vallaris brought sword, shield, or bow with men in support on all sides. Horns sounded on all fronts—long loud horns that bellowed and inspired the defenders. Those behind the walls took shelter and tended animals. Anyone on the wall in support roles quickly sought their nearest way down. The feeling of urgency intensified, and the last of the known worlds, now including Earth, rose to the call.

Everyone from generals to battlefield sergeants knew that morale had to be maintained no matter what. They cheered and clapped to encourage younger ranks, for those that had already seen war knew that fear had an insatiable appetite for courage.

The militia on guard were of the finest fighting caliber—archers of various denomination supported specialists like the Vallaris with their bows and crossbows of old and new. Men in their thousands continued to arrive in support and were welcomed most eagerly in this midnight hour. Those on the line, the ones that manned the wall of all denominations, recognized and respected these new young human leaders who wielded powers unseen before.

There was no pause in the formation of their attackers.

The front lines spread four miles wide, and the first three hundred deep were Borgil. Distinguishing between the dogs and the devils at that distance was difficult at first, but as they edged forwards, it became easier to see the changing lines.

The attack was forming on the front, but they were surely spreading to the flanks.

"They are still a long way off!" Sam cried, but they were moving fast, so fast it seemed unreal. Masses rolled out far and wide: a black hive swarming and spreading both left and right. It brought a shiver down Stacey's spine.

Harry called Sari and Aquiel forward. "Protect the front!" he ordered.

With horns blaring, the Perie obeyed, sending ten thousand Lygard to lead the charge through the north gate and over the drawbridge, taking the battle to their foe.

First blood drawn. The Borgil were no match for them as the Lygard ripped them apart, killing the dogs mercilessly. Flesh tore and blood spattered as friend and foe alike fell when they contacted the second line of the more powerful, sword wielding Grimole, who eventually halted the initial charge.

"Second wave!" Harry was assuming command without ever being asked. He gave orders and nobody questioned him. He was born to lead and to front this campaign.

Another ten thousand Lygard bolstered the first.

"Bow!" Harry yelled.

More horns blasted, and man and Vallaris responded. By bow, crossbow, and the multi-shot Flak, they fired as one. Tens of thousands of arrows and bolts found their target, but their attacker was relentless.

On the east gate, the Xanthu rallied, but the enemy had a clear focus on this sector, perhaps knowing it was a weakness they could exploit. The jungle warriors were courageous, but the

Borgil were merciless, bursting through the gate and carving their way through the lines of animals and men alike.

Pluvius brought about his wizardry, conjuring a storm and downpour—torrential rain that brought flooding, sweeping away hundreds of Borgil.

But their numbers were replaced as quickly as they fell, with mongrels clambering over the bodies of their own kind, as the Allied defense faltered.

Then a lucky shot hit Pluvius. Incredibly, a random arrow had mortally wounded a Uranian.

Harry realized that these underlings were more like Rubezahl as opposed to Remus and Ludwig. Black as midnight, muscular with no wasted fat but not as tall as their master at about five and a half feet, they were proportionate, strong and deadly. With luminous yellow eyes and a rounded pupil like that of a dog, they had the same two fangs with sharp canines on either side. Their bald heads and elongated pointed ears embodied their very existence, for they were bred for war and nothing else.

The Borgil entered the wall, savaging Pluvius—the second Uranian to fall in a millennium. Harry saw the danger and rallied both men and Perie, while looking for Uranians to support their fallen comrade.

"Cover the breach!" he bellowed.

Men flocked to the gate with Perie and a third squadron of ten thousand Lygard beside, using their sonic voices to reverberate inside their enemies' heads until their skulls exploded, forcing them back. But neither side made ground as the Grimole continued to reinforce their fallen. They were innumerable, constantly replacing their dead and continuing to march forever forward.

Regrouping, Mordred was at the wall's edge where he brought to bear fire, with Harry joining and sending both fireballs and long lines of scorching fire along the front lines of the invaders.

The air filled with the stench of death, attracting swarms of flies that crawled over the corpses as the flesh of both man and un-man started to rot.

Sam supported with lightning speed, firing crossbow twenty to thirty a second, burning the cables out one after the other. With a pile of them burned out at his feet, he moved onto the Flak, firing ten times what it was designed to—three hundred and sixty per minute! Of course, the cables of the Flak couldn't cope, and the weapon also burned out; but he had helped turn the tide of this assault, annihilating hundreds of Borgil and Grimole alike.

The gate was secure once more as reinforcements arrived.

It was both a win and a loss, with no one sure who had prevailed.

And it was only the first onslaught.

# Chapter 16


blow to Rubezahl.

Remus and Ludwig were summoned to explain the defeat, but neither had an answer that would satisfy him.

"They are supposed to die, die, yes die," Rubezahl chanted in his foul guttural voice.

His subordinates tried to defend themselves as best they could.

"They have magic, yes magic, flame and fire," Remus answered.

"And new weapons, like magic," Ludwig sobbed.

"Sniveling dogs, dogs yes, dogs, take the west gate now!" Rubezahl ordered without listening.

THE ATTACK WENT WEST WHERE MEN AND LADONIANS WERE stationed, supported by the Vallaris and men to the northeast. Plaga stood ready to defend this world he didn't know, supported by his brothers, as well as other worlds. His satisfied smile showed his pride to front these humans who seemed simple at first, but then proved they were as complex as the cosmos, ready to die for worlds they had never seen.

Harry brought the Royal Guard to the front as mankind once again rose to lead.

The Borgil had suffered many losses in the east but there was no letup, as their oppressor seemed to have an inexhaustible supply of devil and dog.

Flipping his long hair back, a deep humorless laugh boomed as Plaga struck them with disease, afflicting their enemy, who fell victim to viral infection. It was an impressive weapon that stalled the attack and amazed them all. Line after line of Borgil and Grimole fell, leaving those behind faltering in their wake.

Sensing their enemy's decline, men rallied while Vallaris charged with flags flying and horns blasting, holding their attackers at bay and even driving them back.

But just when they thought they were holding their ground, an arrow targeted Plaga, hitting him squarely in the chest.

Stacey was called, and kneeling at his side, she reached out to heal him with vein-like fingers pulsating as she assumed his pain, connecting telepathically. But this was a serious wound, and it proved too much for her. She collapsed from the exertion.

When she woke sometime later in the barracks, Beth was beside her.

"How is he?" she asked immediately.

"Stable, but not completely out of the woods. We think he will be okay, but he will not fight again. You did really well, Stace."

Stacey was able to close her eyes again, content in the thought she had been able to help save him.

The gate remained intact, and it was another bitter-sweet victory, but there was little time to celebrate.

"Cowards, attack the north gate! Cowards take it, yes take it, you take it now and kill them all!" Rubezahl commanded.

Their plan had not progressed the way it was expected, and Remus and Ludwig grew fearful of their Master's wrath, of which they knew too well. He was becoming impatient, but they had little to offer except more Borgil, and more Grimole, for this was all they knew. They joined this third siege on the main north gate, but with some trepidation, for these humans were not like the other worlds they had conquered.

The Uranians were certainly a force to reckon with, given their magic, but one human seemed to be able to read them, to foresee their plans and bring forth soldiers to attack and repel them. They were starting to fear these new adversaries as much as their merciless master.

THE NORTH GATE ATTACK WAS LED BY MANY BORGIL, FOLLOWED by Grimole, and this time with Remus and Ludwig in support, instead of charging from the front, they "led" the charge from the rear. But they also released a new weapon: Gargoyles!

Hundreds and thousands of them flew in great waves like black clouds. They resembled the underlings below except they were smaller, very bony with wings and longer jaws filled with sharp fangs. They swooped in like birds of prey from above, their swiftly flapping wings and screeching deafening as they took their quarry one by one, dropping them from great heights to their deaths.

Morphius supported the cause with the Metamorphan joining them—creatures that changed as they attacked, swapping from animal both known to man, to creatures from other worlds or dimensions unknown. All had razor-sharp teeth, and some were shape shifting, included multiple heads, tearing at the Borgil two at a time while they stabbed a third with their pointed tails and slashed open a fourth or fifth with razor-sharp claws. They were truly a formidable weapon, and Beth joined ranks beside the wizard, who reached out and enabled her to emulate his power.

They worked in tandem, but as fast as their charge took down the enemy, they were replaced, and again their adversary threatened to overrun them. Men, Vallaris, Perie, and Metamorphan all joined together when Harry realized there were simultaneous attacks again on the west and east gates! Orders were issued and executed immediately, without hesitation.

"West gate: Ladonians, 1st Battalion, Vallaris, Mordred!"

"East gate: 2nd Battalion, Perie, Xanthu, Necromancer!"

"North gate: Vallaris, Wazeem, Perie, 3rd Battalion, Morphius!"

But then the news came that Morphius had also fallen to a fatal wound. Without help he became the second Immemorial to fall in this battle and the third Uranian to die in two thousand years.

The allies seemed confident, but just when they thought they were as ready as they could be, the Grimole unleashed yet another new weapon: Rubezahl's elite that he called Borg-riders. Mounted on Borgil, like an apocalyptic cavalry, they wielded their swords from above and slashed their way through the line.

Time and again, humans fell as blades struck, bleeding like slaughtered lambs as those that survived watched on in terror, now wondering if their ability to beat this enemy was beyond them.

Just when all seemed lost, Wazeem and the Royal Guard came from the center, heeding the call as men continued to rally in support, and Perie with Lygard in tow came from the east and Vallaris from the west.

The front lines of the Borgil fell to yet another wave of the combined efforts of Lygard, Perie sonics, and Vallaris bow.

Necromancer was a game-changer, bringing the living dead in their thousands to the aid of all. On the east gate, these walking corpses knew no fear and repelled the attack, simply touching their adversary who disintegrated into piles of dust one after the other and putting the fear of death into those that remained.

Securing the gate, the Ancient moved westward and supported the Vallaris so that they could also shoot down the flying gargoyles in the north, freeing the skies. It worked, and they were then able to do the same on the west gate, helping Mordred. Everyone knew this was not a victory as the enemy kept coming, but for now they remained outside of the wall and that was a win for sure.

Again, there was a feeling of elation, so importantly keeping morale upbeat.

Then something hit Harry. "I know why they came to our dreams," he said aloud. "And how to defeat them."

"Defeat them? How?" Sam asked.

"They come in our dreams to frighten us," Harry said. "Not in real life, but in our dreams, because they are scared of us!" Harry thought he now knew their weakness.

"And how will their fear of us help us defeat them?" Sam was somewhat skeptical; after all they didn't seem too afraid, so far.

"The underlings have no fear, for they are merely puppets of their masters, but Remus and Ludwig are afraid."

"And Rubezahl?" Stacey asked.

"He needs the others, but I have an idea to help with that. Right now, we need the cat's paw," he said mysteriously.

Harry requested Beth to accompany him. It didn't sit well with Sam and Stacey, but they did not push it. After brief good-byes, they left with Rogue and Zeus beside them.

The ride back to the door of the "real" Earth was grueling. Harry would not let up, spurring Beth on, for there was no time to waste. They had to reach the door as soon as possible.

"What does the cat's paw mean?" Beth asked as they walked their horses to rest them.

"It means a person or thing who is used by another to carry out an unpleasant or dangerous task," he said.

"And we are those persons carrying out that dangerous task?" she asked.

"Maybe but not necessarily. It will take great sacrifice, and I'm going to need you to help me with that."

She looked at him and was about to ask for further explanation, but Harry demanded another gallop, and their conversation ended. Their trusted Lygard companions raced to keep abreast, never seeming to tire from the run.

As night began to fall, they reached the door and entered the off-grid room. Beth started to head towards the house, but Harry pulled her back. "No, we go in there," he said, pointing to the recently unblocked wall of the well.

Beth shuddered, but dared not refuse.

They entered the fallen blockade where Harry laid it out for her.

"I'm sending a package to Grimorium, and I need you to slow time for me."

"Slow?" she responded.

"Yes, Beth, you don't stop time. You only slow it to like within a fraction of a millisecond."

"Don't you do that, too?" she asked. "How come you need me?"

"Because I have other tasks to complete," he replied. They locked eyes, and Beth knew there was more that Harry wasn't saying.

There was sadness in those deep blue eyes, and she asked him tentatively, "The cat's paw?"

"Yes, Beth. Forgive me, but the wall, our friends, six worlds, and all of their inhabitants—they all depend on this one moment, this one act of sacrifice, to survive."

"Am I the cat's paw?" she stammered, lip trembling and tears welling, not sure she wanted to hear his answer.

Harry turned and looked at her in astonishment.

"No, Beth!" He took her in his arms, and they hugged. "I just need you to slow time and support me, to stop the flow of these ungodly devils. If we can do that, we will turn the tide, and it will be the end of them."

Beth uttered a sigh of relief but that was short-lived as she watched Harry prepare. First, he took the genie lamp from his knapsack, and then almost, but not quite, clasped his hands, creating an orb that shimmered and sparked between his palms, watching it flame and glow with lightning striking within, like a miniature nova. Immediately neon purple, like bubble gum, he encased it with a cubic force field and placed it inside the genie lamp, which he then returned to the knapsack and zipped closed.

His head lowered, he turned towards the well then looked up to see Beth watching him intently. She gasped, realizing he clearly meant to descend and deliver the bag himself, when Zeus whimpered loudly and seized the bag in his jaws, almost knocking Harry over as he charged his way past before leaping to the well's edge.

"Beth, slow time now!" Harry yelled.

"No!" Beth wailed in response to Zeus as she tried to intercept the leaping Lygard, but he proved too quick for her and disappeared into the darkness below.

"Beth, you have to slow time now! SLOW TIME NOW!" Harry screamed. *"Beth, PLEASE!"*

This time Beth listened, and as time slowed, Harry intervened to also slow Zeus' descent, who reached the chiseled cave floor and entered the luminous green portal glowing ahead of him—a doorway that led to the world of the Grimole invaders, no matter what dimension they might exist on.

Zeus lifted his head high as he sprang through the bridge that separated men and monster.

The noise was muffled, but they felt the explosion like a sonic wave moments later. It shuddered through the humans' hearts and souls above.

"Zeus was the cat's paw," Harry explained. "It was supposed to be me. What I created was a sub-atomic particle that imploded like a black hole, taking Grimorium with it. But even though it had mass, it had no weight—zero gravity."

"That's why someone had to take it there? We couldn't just throw a stone to carry it?" she asked.

"Yes, because it had to go further than just straight down the well. It had to travel along the tunnel to the gateway where the Grimole come from." His lips trembled as he struggled to catch his breath.

"We have Zeus to thank for that," he finished, his voice breaking at last.

Beth burst into tears and hugged him again, sharing his pain.

Then Harry pulled back, his face pale and distraught as he stammered just one word: "Stacey…"

THEY RACED BACK TO THE WALL. THE GAIT OF TRIGGER AND Flicka increased until they galloped at phenomenal speed, with their feet aflame and smoking hoofprints left in their wake.

Beth was amazed and terrified, all at once. Harry had assumed a greater ability now, with his heightened emotions clearly playing a part, extending to Rogue, to their horses, and their speedy return.

Before she knew it, they were at the north gate of the wall and in the in the middle of war, once again.

IN WAZEEM'S ARMS, STACEY LAY BEFORE HARRY, SURROUNDED by Sam, Sari, Aquiel, Issy, Tyla, and twenty of the Royal Guard. An arrow in her chest, her breath shuddered as her color faded.

Wazeem looked at him gravely. "I fear she is too far gone, Master Harry."

Beth burst into tears, and Sam held her, fighting hard to stay strong, but scared to death himself.

Harry knew that Stacey didn't have long. He gently removed the arrow, simultaneously sealing the wound as blood oozed with a lightly glowing hand. Stacey shuddered and groaned loudly. Everyone watched as he reached out to her in the same way Stacey had first done with Flicka and then Plaga, veins popping and blood overtaking his body until he pulsated continuously. His connection was stronger, his power superior, but still it tested him.

Stacey gasped, her chest rising like she was having a heart attack—in shock, but not aware. Harry was struggling, losing strength, throbbing and growing weak too quickly, way too quickly.

But he was determined not to lose her.

More musical lyrics played in his head, something about love getting old or something. The words resonated but he couldn't place them.

The world began to spin, and he feared he would pass out. Memories flooded him: every moment they had spent together first as friends, and then as more than friends. His life with her flashing before his eyes gave him the strength to keep going. Then a single tear dropped from Stacey's eye, rolling down her pallid cheek just as her eyes fluttered open. She gasped, and then gagged as blood trickled from her mouth, looking up to see her go-to guy.

"All I want is you," she barely whispered.

"All I want is you," Harry lulled.

Then Stacey slipped into a peaceful sleep and Harry collapsed, the blue-veined tentacles still pulsating and his body trembling.

# Chapter 17

News of past events spread fast, emerging from inside the wall to Earth and then further. Something dramatic had happened on this world of man. A human had healed one of his own as if he had the power of an immortal, and they had undertaken a mission that had been catastrophic to the enemy—something within the realms of the magic of a Druid.

The mood was euphoric. Humans were now leading the way in this campaign.

Rubezahl knew something wasn't right, but he wasn't sure what. The Grimole had used an old mine shaft linked to the old well at the Porter's garage to enter this world and conquer the puny humans. They were to be the last to stand against him, and then the last few worlds were sure to fall—worlds for his taking, to conquer at will. But the shaft no longer brought forward the underlings from their home world. There was just a light purple-pink glow and silence.

An eerie silence.

He summoned Ludwig who appeared from the shadows, his eyes bulging as he blubbered and trembled in the presence of the wrath of his Master, angering him further.

"You go, go, you go, now!" Rubezahl screeched, splaying his legs and flexing his arms wildly, shaking. "Go. More, bring more yes you bring more or die, yes you die."

Bouncing from one foot to another, his face flushed and wild-eyed, he sneered, for the suffering of others was a malicious pleasure of his.

Ludwig was beside himself. Going down the shaft terrified him, with thoughts of the unknown waiting, but refusal would bring certain death.

Summoning courage, he edged downwards as the depths grew colder and the light grew brighter, becoming a blinding bright pink. His nerve disappeared as fear overcame him the further he delved, finally reaching the gate they had opened to overtake this world; this Earthly world that was to be seized with the few remaining to follow.

But the glow stopped at the gate: there was nothing but complete darkness on the other side.

The gate was locked.

Panic overcame the goblin.

There was no Grimorium on the other side. No more Grimole or gargoyles to come. And there would be no replacements for the slain.

He fled the shaft. Taking to the hills, he howled, scared and alone.

At the wall, the Grimole's forces rallied as the allied defense faltered once again. The invaders shrieked and screamed inhumanely as they attacked again and again, relentless in their desperation to open the wall and expose their enemy.

Inside, the defenders were in danger of defeat yet again as the Grimole continued to attack from all directions. The wall was breached, and they poured in, screaming in jubilation as they slaughtered all in their path.

Stacey remained in the barracks with Beth, Issy, and Tyla, recovering. She was aware how things were going outside, her connection with Harry almost like that of the same mind.

Fearful of defeat, she thought of the Piskies and reached out to Kama, pleading for help, desperate for an answer.

Sam accompanied his brother to the front line of a battlement on the north gate, when he saw a side to Harry he had never seen before: rage.

In one instant Harry felt everything: the murder of his father, the bullying at school, the sheer nerve of the Grimole invading worlds and assuming that these were theirs to conquer, the loss of Zeus; but mostly how it had impacted his family, his loved ones, his Sam, Beth, and Stacey. His fury became fire, and he obliterated the entire front lines of the Borgil. Hundreds burst into flame at once as he let his wrath consume him.

But still they continued to come, relentlessly by the thousand, over-running them again and again without reason, without fear.

On the verge of despair, the Grimole coming at them hard and with renewed enthusiasm, Harry heard Sam shout and followed his gaze to a portal that had magically appeared in the middle of the field. From this portal came creatures that resembled the Grimole with elongated ears, but instead of black skin, they were silver with a striped band of fur running down their spine. By the hundred they came, armed with sword and shield, soaring through the air on flying dog-like creatures.

"They have more coming!" Beth cried in despair, but then the new arrivals carved a path through their enemy, blitzing them.

Astonished, the humans looked on in amazement until one brown and white with an orange streak yelled out, "Hey, Sam!"

This was Ginger, changed for sure now as were their Draggos, mounted up like a six-foot-long steed that could fly, carrying the Piskies like a Pegasus of myth.

"Not the Piskies we knew, but coming here, or the atmosphere, or something else has changed them!" Stacey shouted.

"Whatever it was, they're freaking awesome!" Sam shouted jubilantly.

"Yeah, not so pesky after all!" Beth laughed as she grabbed his arm.

Hundreds became thousands as this new legion helped turn the tide of the war.

Riding a flying dragon-like dog, a Piskie six feet tall, both lean and muscular and with imposing goblin-like features that they recognized as Kama, was then joined by a similarly formidable Piskie-like goblin, his brother Khlama.

"We just added a little water and snacked after midnight!" Kama joked.

Impressed by their arrival, but desperate to now see the end while they held the upper hand, Harry jumped into the fracas outside the wall, charging forward with Wazeem, Sam, and the Royal Guard alongside them with blades aloft, slaying the invading hostiles.

Fearing death from in front and equally from their Masters behind, the Grimole squealed and shrieked.

"No way through!" one shouted.

"We can't win this!" another followed.

"The Masters go, no Masters, no go…" a third cried.

And as the word spread, so did the fear. Like a shockwave from an earthquake, the panic reverberated back through the ranks: a tremor of terror and then the lines broke as they started to flee.

With Ludwig's whereabouts unknown and realizing replacements weren't coming through as he had expected, Remus had to rethink their attack.

Remaining loyal to Rubezahl, he rallied some thousand Borgil and more than five hundred Grimole in another charge, supported by his Master's personal guard: Kruels. They had an exaggerated protruding forehead with serpent eyes and blood-stained lips supporting razor-sharp teeth through which they grunted words of a long-forgotten tongue.

The Kruels were a superior version of Grimole. Rubezahl's sentinel, they were still experimental—but bigger, stronger, and faster. They were bred solely for destruction—the annihilation of any and all that stood against them. They advanced aggressively, fronting Remus in a charge, killing all that stood before them.

Their fighting prowess could not to be denied. First one Royal Guardsman fell, and then another, before a third and fourth became twenty, thirty, and forty as the Grimole elite attacked, seemingly unstoppable.

ON THE OTHER SIDE OF THE BATTLEFIELD, HARRY RALLIED HIS defenses, regrouping to cross the line for what he hoped was their final time.

Leading from the front, he charged forward with Sam and Beth in support, in defense of the belief of freedom, and for their very lives.

More guardsmen fell confronting the Kruels, as their numbers dwindled against this reprisal of their adversary until they were upon them, when Sam beheaded the lead, and Beth, Harry, and Wazeem again attacked. Their advantage on horseback proved too strong with the remaining Royal Guard rallying, taking the day.

With their lines falling, Remus hissed, continuing to laugh in spite of their hopelessness, nonetheless standing forth, rising like a devil.

*Perhaps even the spawn of Lucifer,* Beth thought.

"It thinks it can beat us!" Remus seethed as he accosted Harry, the puny human who had brought about such anguish.

"Wrong, Remus. I know we can beat you, for your numbers have run out. There are no more of your kind coming, for the gate is shut. Now it is your time to die!"

"Ha, you think we are done now? That no more will come? That we just came here on our own, by chance?" Remus replied. "We were told to take your world by the Elders! They opened the gate, and this world is going to be ours, just like all the others!"

Unsure as to what he was saying, Harry stopped. "What the…?" he asked, bewildered.

"Ha, by our own? No, they gave us your world. Your Earth and the other worlds." The Goblin seemed certain of what he was saying.

His mind confused, Harry's anger intensified, and he

answered with fire, but he saw truth in the Goblin's face.

Remus screamed as his body temperature climbed to unbearable levels.

"Behold, Fudo's 300-fold!" Harry seethed, plunging the sword into Remus' belly exposing the Goblin's guts. "For we are not scared of you, nor of your devilish kind!"

The demon fell, burning from the inside out and the blade that pierced him, surprised at how these weaklings could fight back, for they were the Grimole, and this was supposed to be just another world for their taking.

But his dying words remained with Harry, and they worried him.

In the morning, Harry visited Stacey, who was recovering remarkably well. Insistent that she return to duty, Harry relented, knowing her defiance would prove it was always going to be a losing battle anyway.

He told her about the Piskies and their ability to help enable the defeat of the Grimole at last.

She took his hand and asked about Zeus.

"Stace," he said simply, for his look was enough.

She took his hand and held him close.

That night Stacey woke to see Rubezahl leering above

her, growling like a rabid dog with the breath of rotting fish almost strong enough to make her pass out.

Too big, too strong, and too powerful for her to fend off, she was pinned down with beady green eyes and blood-stained lips surrounding razor-sharp fangs dribbling slobber onto her face.

Stacey cringed below the goblin, her chin trembling and body shaking as she whimpered uncontrollably while Rubezahl reveled in her fear.

"You die, yes you does, you die, you die now." He rejoiced seeking vengeance for his fallen army and the worlds that should have been his, for these feeble humans had ruined everything.

But Stacey had played down her renewed strength and brought out her tanto, sliding the knife out of the scabbard and plunging it deep into the demon's belly, sending it back to whatever hell it had come from.

"No, Rubezahl, now you die."

She gasped and slid the dead body off her. It was over.

Finally.

# Chapter 18



THE CELEBRATIONS WERE EXTENSIVE. JUBILANT OFF-WORLDERS joined humans of all races to share in their success. Even the last of the Perie that had remained on their home world joined them now to celebrate the victory.

Everyone was thrilled to see Stacey up and about, but she never ventured far from Harry. The Ladonians greeted Sam and the Scots as true brothers, but Sam noticed Tross was missing.

"He fell in battle," Minor said bitterly, "but he died a warrior's death and his dying words were praise of you, Lad."

Sam felt honored, and they paid respects to Kurkri and Sheelah.

Lachlan McDougal and his clan joined them in celebration of their victory, also toasting their fallen heroes.

The Uranians arrived: Mordred, Necromancer, and Plaga,

who walked proud and with an air of difference, for he no longer seemed afflicted by the suffering of pain and death.

"In fact, I can no longer inflict disease," he told Stacey, taking her hand. "I also never have to feel it, and this is thanks to you, young miss." He looked at her gratefully and spoke with sincerity. "You saved me physically, but you saved me spiritually also."

Stacey smiled and hugged the giant Druid.

Harry, never too far away, looked on with pride. These were now the last three Uranians.

Moreover, he thought of the single Arhmeic remaining as Wazeem joined him—the last of his kind. But the words of Remus continued to haunt him, that the Grimole were told to take Earth by the Uranians. That they opened the gate.

"You conduct yourself like no other Human," Mordred said, interrupting his thoughts. "More like one of us, we think." He paused and Harry waited patiently, but he had a feeling where the topic was going.

The Ere did not disappoint him. "You have the potential to become a Guardian."

Feigning surprise, Harry asked him outright, "Really? Tell me, Mordred, did you lead the Grimole to us, to engage us in this universal war?" He knew his voice betrayed his bitterness, but he continued anyway. "To Earth where we would have no choice but to fight or die?"

"And did you take away any option except to go and help the Piskies?"

Mordred considered his answer as he weighed up the human before him. "You are creatures of some ability, intelligence, and you have potential. We encouraged the enemy, yes, we enticed them, until they swallowed the baited hook and brought about your assistance. That in turn brought about help from the other known worlds including the Piskies, but that door was opened by another." He was matter of fact like he was quoting a newspaper article, rather than talking about their possible global annihilation.

"By Wazeem?" Harry guessed.

"Indeed. This opportunity opens to only a few virtually ever, but the offer is there for you to become one of us, an Elder no less," Mordred finished.

Harry knew the conversation was done.

Later he discussed it with Stacey.

"I get the honor that it suggests," he started, "but it's kind of old-world now, you know what I mean?"

"Your magic has surpassed them." It wasn't a question.

"I guess so." He sighed heavily and shook his head. "I don't want to disrespect them, but I can't agree with what they did. I can hardly believe it, really." He paused, and Stacey waited patiently for him to continue, knowing his difficulty to say the words.

"It's like he was prepared to sell us out, at whatever cost. He was hedging his bets both ways, almost as if it didn't matter who won, as long as it ended." His voice cracked in disbelief as he stared at the floor, feeling that they had all been used.

"Like we were really the cat's paw, even."

Stacey reached out and linked his fingers in hers, a metaphorical hand on his heart, in empathy.

She looked into his eyes with affection, continuing to wait.

After a short silence, Harry continued. "Besides," he said, staring into the deepest depths of her beautiful brown eyes, "I have other plans."

THE NEXT FEW DAYS WERE TOUGH FOR ALL. THE TEENS VISITED as many as they could who had worked, fought and lost kin in this epic battle to free them all, paying their respects to families grieving their losses.

The Perie had lost many of their female guard and so many more of their beloved Lygard. Everyone was dismayed to hear Aquiel had perished during the final hostilities. The girls hugged Sari who was clearly devastated, along with her cousin and daughter.

"Victory comes with great loss," Harry said regretfully. "Bittersweet is the knowledge of how we have triumphed. It's not just another battle like the last one on Valeo, but now the end to a war that has spanned generations."

Now, they could all plan to rebuild their lives without fear for the first time in almost two thousand years.

Tyla had assumed her cousin's role of leading Counsel to the Queen, a little subdued but focused, and aware of the responsibilities of this new role.

Issy was now in training to one day assume the crown, seeming more mature and having experienced war first hand. She appeared more collected, grounded and amicable.

Sari was clearly feeling the loss of her sister the most. Understandably grieving their losses, she was nevertheless moving on with true Royal spirit, for the Perie had always assumed the mantle of responsibility. They knew that although their crown did not extend to other worlds, they were obliged to offer assistance nonetheless.

Harry welcomed the Perie accompaniment, for their support was reciprocal.

Voicing his observations, the teens elected to stay with the Perie for a few more days, sharing food, conversation, and everything from magic to weapons, and song—lots of song.

It was a good decision, with time well-spent, and when they eventually left, the bond between them was cemented forever.

The sisterhood regrouped and planned their new Lygard breeding program, promising ancestral offspring of Zeus to Harry and lineal heritage to Rogue, Belle, and Deuce.

The offer was unparalleled and their goodbyes were simply "until we meet again."

Saying goodbye to the Piskies was in some ways harder for them, especially for Stacey, who had bonded so intimately. Kama had become like family.

They spent another few days riding the wall, paying tribute to those who assisted in the victory, accepting their acclaim and reliving the fight of their lives. Because of the hype rather than in spite of it, the idea of reclusion became very appealing. In a rare moment alone, Stacey asked Harry what he meant by "other plans."

"Well, I was thinking of joining the Priesthood…"

Stacey laughed, something he hadn't heard in a long time. He had missed it without even realizing it. It was a sad thought, but he was going to do something about it for sure.

Then Harry told Stacey what he had been thinking.

"I want to travel."

"Oohh, me too!" She jumped on that.

"But not Japan, Greece, or Egypt," he said. "I want to travel the galaxy, and then the universe."

She gasped in apprehension.

"It's a big deal, I know, but I can open doors to worlds that are still unknown. We can start with the Piskies, the Perie, Ladon, Valeo, and Xanthus—worlds and friends we know."

"And then move on to other, um, unknown worlds?" she asked.

"Sure," Harry said. "There will be many. Want to come with me?"

She gave him her million-dollar smile.

"Marco," she said.

"Polo," he answered.

They both laughed and hugged.

Of course, there was never any question that Sam and Beth would not be invited. And no question that they wouldn't accept that invitation. Sam tried to play hard to get, but Beth wasn't having any of it.

"Visit new worlds, meet old friends, help keep Sam on the straight and narrow," she said.

"Skip school, ooh yeah!" He laughed. That was the Sam they knew and loved.

The others joined in laughing, and their excitement snowballed, exhilarated at the prospect of the future. They had evolved and grown together, defeating an overwhelming enemy despite enormous odds.

But Harry knew the power they had assumed was at a cost, for they seemed to have lost something—their sense of being their true selves. They lost their laughter, enjoyment in life, and their youth.

Harry wasn't prepared to let that go.

Wazeem smiled, recognizing his Master's choice, for this was the human spirit, and it was this that he now understood—and admired.

Harry approached the Jinni. He now stood only a mere two inches shorter, and it was as if they had known each other their entire lives.

"Of course, we expect you will join us."

"No, Master, I don't think I should burden you further," Wazeem answered. "I shall probably join the Druids on Urania now."

"No, Wazeem, we say you should accompany us on our holiday, and I will not hear any argument about it," Stacey joined in.

"What is a holiday, Mistress Stacey?"

"Well, that's time abroad, Wazeem," Beth answered.

"Abroad, Mistress Beth? I do not understand." He was quite befuddled.

"Boardies! Beaches! Babes! Oops, I meant beach balls," Sam burst out, copping a look from Beth.

Now Wazeem looked really confused, but Harry put his hand on his arm.

"I spoke to Mordred. He said you were the one that brought about our involvement with the Piskies. I reckon they changed the course of things. That you did. Now we just want you to join us for a good time, my friend."

That was enough for Wazeem. He remembered their very first meeting—the offer of friendship.

"You just have to lose the Master routine," Harry said wryly.

THERE WERE NO GOODBYES AT HOME. NONE WERE NEEDED AS time would merely slow, and their families would not even be aware they had been gone. Time had no meaning, which was both an exhilarating and scary thought. They still took time for hugs, especially with Regina, albeit while trying to act nonchalant, as if they were heading to the shops in town.

With Rogue, Belle, and Deuce at their sides, they headed off.

*Not by plane or boat,* Stacey thought, *but by a wish of the Harry Portal, LOL.*

FROM DEEP WITHIN THE BOWELS OF THE EARTH, LUDWIG WALlowed in self-pity.

"Where's the Master, the Rubezahl, where's the Master?" he asked himself aloud in a whiny, grating voice, chasing small rodents, all alone in the darkness.

"Theys beat us," he replied to himself, seething with anger.

"The humans beats us, theys beats us," he wailed.

"Not yet, no." His master's voice echoed off the cavern walls.

Ludwig looked up in surprise, shocked and fearful, wondering how this could be real.

"But hows, Master? Hows?" he asked.

Rising before him, Rubezahl's massive wings unfolded, as he again resembled images of the Devil incarnate, self-absorbed in his own glory.

"Only in their dreams. Not dead, no. Just a dream!" The goblin laughed.

# Acknowledgments

I'd like to acknowledge the time, effort, and input from P. J. (Tricia) Hoover who did more than edit and assist with publishing this book, but got right into the story and helped shape it to become the work it is today. Thank you so much, Tricia. I look forward to our next venture!

# About the Author

Kieran McNamara was the youngest of nine children born into a loving family that struggled in a small town. He escaped into fiction at a young age, but pursued a career in business before turning to writing.

He lives a quiet life with his wife Keri, close to his children.

www.ingramcontent.com/pod-product-compliance
Lightning Source LLC
Chambersburg PA
CBHW071156180726
48291CB00007B/2479